THE
FUTURE
OF
MISBEHAVIOR

2033

THE

FUTURE

OF

MISBEHAVIOR

INTERPLANETARY DATING, MADAME PRESIDENT, SOCIALIZED PLASTIC SURGERY, AND OTHER GOOD NEWS FROM THE FUTURE

FROM THE EDITORS OF NERVE.COM
INSTIGATED BY SVEDKA

CHRONICLE BOOKS
SAN FRANCISCO

Library of Congress Cataloging-in-Publication Data:

2033 : the future of misbehavior : interplanetary dating, Madame President, socialized plastic surgery, and other good news from the future
/ by the editors of Nerve.

   p. cm.

ISBN-10: 0-8118-5940-1

ISBN-13: 978-0-8118-5940-0

1. Short stories, American. 2. Erotic stories. 3. Science fiction,
American. 4. Satire, American. I. Nerve.com (Computer file) II. Title.

  PS648.S47A612 2007

  813'.01083538—dc22

                     2006030991

MANUFACTURED IN CANADA

DESIGNED BY JACOB T. GARDNER

SET IN **BEMBO** AND FOUNDRY GRIDNIK

SVEDKA VODKA IS A REGISTERED TRADEMARK OF SPIRITS
MARQUE ONE LLC.

DISTRIBUTED IN CANADA BY RAINCOAST BOOKS

9050 SHAUGHNESSY STREET

VANCOUVER, BRITISH COLUMBIA V6P 6E5

10 9 8 7 6 5 4 3 2 1

CHRONICLE BOOKS LLC

680 SECOND STREET

SAN FRANCISCO, CALIFORNIA 94107

WWW.CHRONICLEBOOKS.COM

CONTENTS

INTRODUCTION

BY NERVE.COM

.

Once, in the not-so-distant past, the promise of the not-so-distant future seemed clear.

Thanks to our flying cars and single-traveler jet packs, traffic congestion would be relegated to the dustbin of history, along with hunger, plague, and the forty-hour workweek. Robot maids in anachronistic uniforms would clean our homes (if our homes didn't clean themselves), distribute our food pellets, and anticipate our every whim. We would name our children things like Astra and Zephrox, dress them in unisex smocks that would change color according to their mood or hydration level, and take them out for a wholesome dinner at the restaurant on the rings of Saturn, where we would feast on dishes such as Betelgeuse Burgers and Mom's Meat Loaf Galactica. Humankind's baser impulses, after millennia of greed and violence, would be held firmly in check. Money would be obsolete (at least according to *Star Trek*), as would most recognizable sexual congress (again, *Star Trek;* though Captain Kirk might have exchanged a tongueless kiss with the alien slave girl who writhed lasciviously at his feet, intercourse seemed to be achieved mainly through a sort of brief and tortuous mind meld), thus eliminating the need for messy and unsightly gels and pessaries. Racism and intolerance would vanish, and the universe, save for a few power-hungry extraterrestrial warlords, would be at peace.

Yet here we are, more than half-finished with the first decade of the twenty-first century, walking on sidewalks firmly tethered to the actual ground, naming our kids Connor and Mackenzie, and—unless we (a) live with our parents or (b) married well—scrubbing the toilet our own damn selves. If the restaurant on the rings of Saturn exists, it is not on the actual rings of an actual planet, but in one of two places, one of which requires a PayPal transaction of $75 to a teenager in Osaka to enter, while the other is sandwiched between Space Mountain and the video arcade in the Magic Kingdom.

Sex and money, however, seem to be at an all-time high in popularity. And by "all-time high," we mean at levels of public obsession unseen since the time of the Roman Empire (we think; contrary to popular belief, we haven't been around that long).

The moment a sniffling starlet is caught sans knickers, we sit glued to our computers, ogling and then debating the veracity of her lady parts. The Internet (a dizzying construct not even dreamed of by Space Age prognosticators) has made pundits of us all, it's true, but has also ensured that in the new millennium no pervert shall be left behind. Even the moral watchdogs of the right are in on the action, gleefully describing coupling techniques of homosexuals for the viewers at home in language more Marquis de Sade than Moral Majority, FCC be damned. Money, it's better to not even get started on, lest we throw ourselves out the window of our shockingly overpriced apartment before we finish writing this paragraph. Suffice it to say that, while we may be hoping to earn enough this year to warrant a W-2 form, thanks to an ever-vigilant Fourth Estate we can tell you how much Jessica Simpson dropped on her last trip to Kitson and assess with reasonable accuracy the major assets of Ron Perelman, as well as all the tax he isn't paying.

But self-pity is so 2004. Money is fun! Sex is fun! And so are the things one uses money to buy in order to more easily obtain sex, such as fashionable clothing, alcohol, and drugs. Add to this a dash of bitterness, a pinch of envy, and a smattering of frantic paparazzi, and if you don't hear some house music (or whatever your personal approximation of it may be) thumping in your head, you might seriously consider letting the TiVo catch *Project Runway* and leave the house some night this week.

The world of nightlife is arguably one of the most forward-thinking businesses there is; impresarios and denizens alike are

moving constantly, like sharks, on the unending quest for the
Next Big Thing, and the Next Next Big Thing, and the So Much
The Next Big Thing That Only Fifteen People In Glasgow
Know About It Thing, leaving the rest of us behind at the Last
Big Thing, as redundant and forgotten as rejected bits of forlorn
knitwear on the last day of a Barneys warehouse sale. So, never
ones to shy away from a challenge, we asked some of our most
forward-thinking literary voices to beat the trendsetters and
beautiful people (in some cases, they may overlap) at their own
game and lay out visions of 2033.

What they have predicted may surprise you. It's a world both
reassuringly familiar—Earth is still, for the most part, inhabitable;
people still take mass transit and buy things frequently—and
interestingly alien, literally and figuratively. Some writers have
followed our glossy, media-saturated culture to its next logical
steps: plastic surgery is subsidized by the government; a nonprofit
hands out grants to the tabloid fodder of tomorrow; suburban
dads rent teams of paparazzi by the hour; and a man becomes a
billionaire selling celebrities' trash on the Internet. They explore
mid-twenty-first-century sexual politics in provocative terms
both figurative (a female boss sexually harasses her hot himbo
of an employee) and literal (Madame President's First Lady, rest-
less on the campaign trail, gets up to a bit of mischief with a
bosomy staffer). Our present ideas of marriage and relationships
are challenged and stretched, as a women's magazine urges brides
to get excited about their weddings, despite the 100 percent

divorce rate; ever-increasing longevity leaves septuagenarians to cavort like sorority pledges on spring break; America emerges from a long, dark period of Orwellian, federally enforced Puritanism when organized swinging overtakes baseball as the official national pastime; and an enterprising tranny presents a comprehensive plan for the resleazification of that longtime symbol of all that is Good and Wholesome: Times Square.

And of course, what would the future be without some sci-fi gadgetry and outer-space adventures? We've got that too, as online dating takes an intergalactic turn, and a loutish Romeo considers an upgrade on his state-of-the-art robot girlfriend.

If this collection is any indication, and if we aren't all living underground or crowded on the last inhabitable patch of desert in what was once known as North Dakota, 2033 will be an interesting (and damn sexy) year. But in the meantime, take a night off from the clubs; grab a can of your favorite electrolyte-rich, performance-enhancing super-beverage (or, as we prefer, a refreshing vodka cocktail); and spend some time in the future. And then, we suggest, put this book in a time capsule, to be opened twenty-seven years from now, when howls of derisive laughter at its very quaintness will surely haunt its fuddy-duddy authors in their hyperbaric chambers through the remaining years of their lives.

Enjoy!

TABLOIDS BRING BACK FAMILY VALUES!

BY ANA MARIE COX

2033

FUTURE

MIS-

Jim tapped his fingers on the steering wheel of his Hummer H12 (seats two). He was going to be late for work. He looked toward the front door, and he imagined that he could see the ivy trembling on its trellis from the force with which Marcia had slammed the door.

Why do we keep having the same fight over and over? he thought, replaying it in his head:

MARCIA: If you want a whore, get a whore! Don't just screw the nanny!

JIM: Well, maybe if you weren't so busy putting God-knows-what up your nose, you'd have the energy to screw me yourself!

MARCIA: You'd like it if I got fat again, wouldn't you?

JIM: I didn't marry you for your body.

MARCIA: No, you married me for my money! My money that pays for the goddamn nanny!

JIM: You won't have any money left if you keep that habit up.

MARCIA: If I stop, I'll balloon.

And so on. *Whore-coke-fat-money-whore-fat-coke-money.* Sometimes she called him gay. But he basically had it memorized. The Clarks down the street—now, they had some good, original fights. Abortions, plastic surgery gone wrong, sex tapes... *Would anyone notice if we stole the bit about driving around with the baby in his lap?* He wondered if anyone wrote their material.

Glancing toward the monitor in his dashboard, Jim saw a small spike in the number of users searching "Jim Marcia Stevenson fucking nanny." Finally! What was the nanny's name again? Fuck, he should have mentioned it. Whatever—she was with the kids in the country anyway.

His cell phone buzzed: "im wet 4 you darling." He smiled and thumbed a message back: "keep urself amused 4 awhile . . . fyl."

A van bearing the logo PAPA-RENT-ZI pulled up to the curb and began disgorging a small phalanx of photographers and at least a couple of guys with handheld video cameras. Jim put the car in reverse and waited for them to rush the miniature SUV. The click and whirr of the cameras sounded muffled. *Forgot to roll down the window. Jesus, it's that kind of day,* thought Jim, lowering the tinted glass on both sides. He was just beginning to extend his palm, "No, guys, really, no, can't comment . . ." when they all heard a sharp report from down the block.

Jim whipped his head around. The photographers rushed to the other side of the H12: "Hey, it's Bill Simmons, and he's in a dress! With a gun!" The brigade hurdled Jim and Marcia's hedge, press tags flying behind them.

Jim gritted his teeth as he watched them go. *I should have known a time-share wasn't going to work,* he said to himself. He gunned the engine and fishtailed out of the driveway, not really looking where he was going. *Hell,* he thought, *if I'm lucky maybe I'll hit someone.* But he shuddered at the thought: *Slow-moving car chases are so over.*

Stuck in traffic on the way to his office, Jim put the car into Auto-Crawl and stretched the monitor to full windshield size. Another text message waited for him: "cant wait." "As soon as I get 2 work," he responded. His brief pop of pleasure at the thought was dampened by what he saw on the larger screen. Bill's stunt was all over Channel Cherrydale: "Simmons snaps!" read the crawl under the footage of Bill lumbering through his wife's azaleas, wearing the dress Jim recognized from the annual Northern Virginia Near Suburbs Small Screen Reality Awards last April. "Will Bad Billy be able to bring back his bride after this break with reality?" *Right,* Jim thought, *Claire had left Bill for her manicurist.* A pop-up ad in the corner of the screen asked Jim if he wanted to buy a copy of the printed shift Bill wore on his rampage.

Irritated, Jim flipped channels. FallsChurchNow carried a wrap-up of who in the neighborhood had become a Scientologist recently. NWDC—which covered the Connecticut Avenue corridor of Washington—was profiling the lawyer who drew up "beard" agreements for Dupont Circle residents. All old news, all boring. The Bill Simmons story could bubble through to the entire metro area. Unless someone bought an ultrasound or led a freeway chase, Simmons was a lock for the whole news cycle. Back on Channel Cherrydale, a mug shot of Simmons flashed, his hair wild and his eyes fixed in a studied blank stare that Jim knew had to be the work of a life coach.

"Dial rep," Jim sighed. The car dialed, and a perky automated voice answered smoothly: "Wendell, Marks, and Sloane. We treat you like the star you are! How can I help you?"

"Patty Ewing, please."

"And whom can I say is calling?"

"Jim Stevenson."

"And this is regarding representation, placement, a lawsuit, or rehab escort service?"

"Representation."

The car's speakers burbled as the computer patched him through to Patty. "Jim! It's been an age! How are you doin', sweetheart? Marcia and you looked just great at the Safeway opening last week. Is she showing? Is she?"

"What's wrong with your voice, Patty?"

"Oh!" A quick burst of static came, followed by Patty again, her voice dropped an octave or two and thickened with smoke: "What can I do for you, honey? You still screwing around on that beautiful wife of yours?" That was better. If he'd wanted a California smoothie, he'd have asked for one. Jim liked Patty's overt abrasiveness—it reminded him of some movie he saw once about agents.

"Yeah, I've got something going with the nanny. Did you get the sex tape I sent you?"

Traffic crawled forward. Jim called up the digital file of him and the nanny—what was her name, dammit?—and watched it on mute. The graininess added a touch of realism, though it meant you couldn't really see her lips move around his cock. But it had been expensive enough to make without pouring even more money into CGI.

"It looks great, Jim, really. I'll leak it when I get a chance . . ." Patty trailed off.

"Bill Simmons is killing us." Jim pulled into a parking space at work.

"I have to say, sweetheart, that all these gags are good, but they *reeeeeeek* of the pros, you know? You have to come up with something new, something genuinely spontaneous." He heard a sharp inhale off of a cigarette: "Have either of you ever thought about doing it with a dog?"

"What?"

"Just blue-skying here, Jim. Maybe the dog could just watch . . ."

Jim rolled his eyes. "Let's just stick with the sex tape for now, Patty."

"I'm sure it'll be fine. It's fuzzy, but she looks twelve. That'll help."

They signed off. In the parking lot, his colleagues meandered among the thicket of cars, most with cell phones plugged to their ears or a screen of some kind winking up from their upturned palms. Jim wondered how many of them were simply digesting their own Google alerts and was struck by an idea: *Wonder how Patty would like footage of me masturbating in public?*

His own cell jangled with more text messages: "coffee break, yes? I have the cream . . . hotel down the street. 432." He felt a rush of blood to his thighs and did a quick U-turn in the parking lot, glancing around to make sure people were checking messages and not him.

It was hard to keep a grin off his face. Thinking about the date made the back of his neck prickle pleasurably. In the lobby, he asked for directions for the public restroom and then, on the way to it, he spied the rent-a-razzi. *Fucking hell,* he said to himself, *never around when you need them, and now . . .*

He laid low behind a ficus and considered his options. He was contemplating doing a house paging call for Simmons when a lithe blonde in a trench coat and large sunglasses stepped out of the elevator. At first, the 'razzi didn't seem to notice her, but she stopped and looked over her sunglasses at them, subtly flashing her monthly membership pass. They went nuts. She pulled her trench tighter around her as they trailed, popping, flashing, screaming for more.

Jim breathed again. He ducked into the stairwell and arrived on the fourth floor flushed, huffing slightly, *Patty, Bill, what's-her-face* all distant memories. His knock was answered quickly, but he couldn't avoid making sure the hall was empty.

A woman's hand pulled him in. He started to protest: "Baby, you know we can't keep taking these kind of chances. I almost ran into a camera crew on my way upstairs."

"Shhh, honey," Marcia said, smiling. "No one will ever know."

THE PARIS HILTON INTERNATIONAL FELLOWSHIP

BY RACHEL SHUKERT

2033

FUTURE

MIS-

The halcyon days of Studio 54, nearly a half-century ago, must seem endearingly quaint to the jaded Manhattan revelers of today—a simpler, more innocent time when, despite the legendarily draconian door policy, an enterprising art student armed with baby oil, a Bedazzler, and an aura of sexual availability might charm his or her way past the velvet rope to exchange pleasantries and bodily fluids with the rich, thin, and famous.

The clubs today may be thick with celebrities, but the famous, while sought after, are hardly a successful club owner's bread and butter. Rather, it is the little people—the anxious investment bankers, the minor gangsters, the nameless Europeans, and the middling socialites who populate the outer tables near the door and the downstairs dance floor—that are any successful club owner's meal ticket, and, thus far, the business model of keeping the VIPs pampered and the peasants subjugated has worked beautifully.

But times have changed. Rising rents and overhead have driven prices up. An executive managing director of sales who might have sprung for a $600 bottle of champagne twenty-five years ago is unlikely to spend the tens of thousands of dollars the same bottle would run him today. At nightspots these days, one no longer needs merely a platinum card—one needs a card made out of actual platinum.★

The dearth of civilian participation in today's nightlife also poses an important philosophical problem. Without nonfamous clubgoers to exclude from VIP areas, cut in front of in bathroom lines, and occasionally engage in hasty, anonymous sexual intercourse with, how can a celebrity truly feel like a celebrity? In a club of only celebrities, do celebrities cease to exist?

In 2030, several prominent nightlife impresarios, hoping to restore the crucial imbalances of wealth and social status in their clubs, formed the New York State Federation of the Night (NYSFN) and joined with the Lionel Richie Family, longtime philanthropists and arbiters of cool, to form the $500 million

---

★ Offered by Visa, for a limited time, the Genuine Platinum Emperor card not only offers an unlimited line of credit but is also now the only card accepted by all LVMH/Bernard Arnault retailers, the human-trafficking industry, and the People's Republic of China.

Nicole Richie Memorial Nightlife Endowment, which annually awards several sizable fellowships to deserving candidates with special aptitude, promise, or passion in the field of clubbing. The grants, named for the Richie Family scion who died tragically of "exhaustion" in 2015, are to be spent at the recipient's discretion, though he or she is required to report periodically to the board of trustees to detail how the monthly allowance has been spent and report any really serious celebrity gossip he or she has accu-

mulated thereby.

"Nicole was a precious rainbow, and since her death, we've wanted to do something that would commemorate what she stood for," said a frail Lionel Richie from Santa Barbara, Cali-

fornia, where he is in hospice. "She loved being famous more than anything, and I know that she would have wanted us to do everything in our power to keep being famous special. God bless my baby, wherever she is."

Grants awarded include the following:★★

The Nicole Richie Memorial "Angel" Fellowship: This is the largest of the grants. It is awarded on the basis of personal style, physical fitness, personality, and sartorial sophistication. Weekly weigh-ins are required of the recipient, whose weight,

---

★★ No dollar amounts are ascribed here, as that would be tacky.

regardless of height, is not to exceed 103.2 pounds (46.8 kilograms). Special preference is given to candidates with a proven interest in ballet, figure skating, fashion design, creative writing, or entomology.

The Paris Hilton International Fellowship: Shortly before her death, Nicole reconciled with Paris Hilton after a ten-year feud, and in the spirit of peace, Lionel Richie chose to name a grant after his beloved daughter's childhood friend and longtime rival. A weak but enthusiastic Nicole even helped plan the grant's criteria. The Paris is reserved for candidates who are struggling to overcome a physical obstacle, such as a lazy eye, developmental delays, or severe genital herpes. The fellowship lasts for one year, and ends with a one-way ticket to the Greek islands, from which the recipient is required to arrange/fund his or her own return.

The Lindsay Lohan Biennial Scholarship: This very special prize is awarded to candidates from a troubled family situation. Candidates must also exhibit special talent in the performing arts, with an emphasis on dance, and show a keen interest in the industrial economies of developing nations, particularly those in South America. Upon learning of the endowment in her name, Ms. Lohan was reached for comment at her home in Bahrain, where she lives with her third husband, Sheik Omar Abdullah Haziz al-Saud.

"It's not for some college thing, is it? No? Good," said the thrilled Academy Award winner. "Because I didn't go to college."

The Nicky Hilton Prize: Awarded to candidates who exhibit special promise in the handbag arts. Applicants must be eighteen or over. Recipients are selected on the basis of an interview and an assessment of qualifications, including charm, poise, personality, personal style, and appearance in photographs, among others.

A personal essay is also required with each application. Here are some excerpts from past winners:

"Nicole Richie is my idol for many reasons, and I can think of nothing in the whole wide world that would make me more incredibly full of pride and would be such an amazing and superlative experience than to truly follow in her footsteps as a fashion icon and tastemaker for my generation . . . her miraculously extraordinary sense of personal style is an amazingly incredible inspiration to me when making my own fashion choices . . . like Nicole, I have suffered from a lot of people being jealous of me, but I don't let them get me down. They can just go about their own lame little ways, because I know that I am destined to be a true star, just like Nicole's star shone so brightly through the night until it was finally extinguished. I guess some of us just shine too brightly, but we have to seize the day when we can and not let life pass us by, because our time here is short and we have to live it to the utmost, fullest extent. I think Madonna said it best in this really sad old movie I saw on TCM the other day where she plays this beautiful Latina woman who marries the president and right before she dies of cancer of some kind she sings:

'The choice was mine, and mine completely

I could have any prize that I desired

I could burn with the splendor of the brightest fire

Or else, or else I could choose time'

I think Nicole knows what that means, and I do, too . . . also, like Nicole, I am very, very committed to physical fitness."

—Tallulah Jade Anderson, Tarrytown, NY

"I have overcome SO many truly difficult difficulties in my life, like dyslexia and being a natural brunette, but I have overcome them with flying colors, as I mentioned earlier, and that is why I think I should be the next Paris Hilton International Fellow . . . I am a hot bitch, and I absolutely bring 110 percent to every party I go to, whether I am working or just there for fun, and when I say I am a bitch, I mean like a sexy, fierce female, not like 'bitch' in a negative way, because I am a super-nice and considerate person and everyone who really knows me says so. You can call them if you want—I'll give you the code to my Sidekick XXXVII later, and you can get their numbers. One example of how I am really nice is that I don't just want this money to launch my career as a model/actress/author/entrepreneur. Well, that's part of it, but the real reason I want to do all those things is to build a better life for London Punani Aniston Metzler, who is the baby I am raising, ALL BY MYSELF. Isn't that the hottest name? He is from Botswana, which is in Africa, and I got him in my goody bag at the Swarovski party last year, where I was just some guy's plus-one but still talked my way into the deluxe goody bag, which ought to tell you something about my 'potential' in this field. Also, I am excited to take him to Greece, where he can be around other people who are 'swarthy' and won't feel like a total freak all the time."

—Tori Olivia Metzler, Montecito, CA

"My parents divorced shortly after my first birthday, and I have seen very little of my father since. For most of my life, I have been the sole caregiver of my clinically depressed mother. In the past, this was less of a burden, but after undergoing hip-replacement surgery five years ago, she has grown very heavy and is no longer particularly mobile.

As my mother was once a famous beauty, the ravages of time, illness, and (we might as well face it) Big Macs on her looks have been quite difficult for her to handle emotionally. I love my mother very much—we were extremely close when I was a boy—and I didn't mind caring for her at first, but time and her increasingly severe mental illness have worn me down. I do her shopping, keep her doctor's appointments, regulate her medication, and manage her finances, only to receive abuse in return, particularly on this last count.

My mother, a wealthy woman, was horribly taken advantage of financially by my father, and as a result has become terribly paranoid about money. She accuses me of stealing from her, of being 'just like HIM,' and berates me with a litany of my father's financial follies: $300,000 for a diamond-encrusted five-iron, $15,000 for a baby shark that he forgot to feed, $75,000 for a vintage bottle of champagne he was photographed sharing with a stripper at the MGM Grand in Vegas.

I cannot so much as mention that I could use a new pair of sneakers or that we might consider hiring some cleaning help once a week, let alone requesting some capital to strike out on my own. I am desperate to get out of here, ladies and gentlemen of the board, and I feel that the Lindsay Lohan Biennial Scholarship might be my only escape.

I am also anxious to flee to more tolerant pastures, if you get my meaning. Mama has grown very religious in recent years, and when she came across me in my room innocently lip-synching to some old Xtina songs the other day, she became irate, and not for the obvious reasons.

'Makeup artists are faggots!' she shouted, her chins wobbling. 'Backup dancers are faggots! Not no son of mine!'

I felt it would be aggravating the situation to mention that my father had been a backup dancer when they met. Instead, I pointed out that things have changed, that gay marriage is now legal in 47 states.

'Not in Louisiana, it ain't! And thank fucking God for that!' she cried, and sped away down the hallway. If her motorized cart could have left rubber tracks on the shag carpet, it would have.

Please get me out of here. All I want is a chance to come to New York, dance to some house music, have some anal sex, and get my picture in a few magazines again, and God, as my Grandma Lynne says, will take care of the rest."

—Sean Preston Federline, Kentwood, LA

Entries for this year must be postmarked no later than August 24, 2033. Recipients for 2034 will be announced by December 15.

THE UPGRADE

BY KARL IAGNEMMA

2033

FUTURE

MIS-

Things were pretty good until 2033.

In fact, things were really good until 2033. I was living in Pasadena in those days. The weather was a weird, wonderful joke. I was twenty-five, hanging on to some leftover muscle from USC, driving a '31 Chevy Stallion, and spending weekends in a haze of Stim. I was still doing the assistant manager thing at Robo-Maxx, but the hours were decent and the employee discount truly rocked—15 percent off neuro upgrades, 30 percent off mech mods, 30 percent off cosmetic mods. My apartment was on the bombed-out end of Colorado Boulevard, but it was huge and the rent was comical and my neighbor was a shy, lovesick vegan named Grace, who, every Sunday, would bake cranberry muffins and bring a platter over for Katrina and me to nibble. (And she really nibbled—I'd had a refurbished stomach mod installed on her the previous August.)

Weird, wonderful days. I hadn't dated a woman—a human— since 2025. Susanna, with the dimples and nose hair, the half-insane laugh, the daddy issues. Oh, Susanna. She'd stood on her chair at Bella Vita and thrown a dirty napkin in my face and said that my soul was ruined. She'd said that I was psychologically retarded, that I was as emotionless as a bot.

So the thing was, I didn't miss women. I didn't miss the child-ish flirting, the stupid expensive gifts, the ridiculous countdown to sex—and then the endless phone calls and v-chats, the passive aggres-sion, the pitiful obsession with money, money, money. How could I miss women? I had my job, I had my apartment, and I had Katrina.

In the mornings, after I left for work, Katrina would do her recharge thing, then mop the floors and scrub the spotless tub, disinfect the toilet, iron my pit-stained undershirts. In the evenings she'd cook dinner—pasta and Mexican and simple stir-fries, since I'd never bothered with a cooking upgrade—and afterward I'd flop on the sofa with a Stim and Katrina would start a swaying, hum-ming striptease, her skin caramel-colored and glossy, scarless. She'd flick her G-string at me with her big toe, and she'd giggle. Pretty soon I'd command her over and we'd get started, me with one eye on the holo, Katrina with her eyes pinched shut and hair whipped into a nest, until eventually she'd look at me with a coy, catlike grin. "You should finish," she'd whisper. "My power is pretty low."

"Flip over," I'd say. "Position thirteen. Activity level high."

Of course she had 1500 SPI skin and Sugaku touch sensors. She had actual human hair—Indonesian hair, from the lowlands outside Jakarta—and human eyebrows, human lashes. A Bose voice box that let her sing like a soprano, growl like a convict, or moan like a desperate virgin. She had top-end MicroMo servomotors, electroactive actuators in the soft, sensitive places.

And of course she was gorgeous. I'd spec'd her out as a cross between Irina Porozka and Ginger Newton, with grace notes from the old-school beauties: Hayworth, Monroe, Loren, Jolie. But her fingers were ten millimeters longer than factory spec, her eyes three millimeters wider. She was better than human: more beautiful, crushingly beautiful. Even the hard-core modders at RoboMaxx held their breath when she strolled past.

I don't know why I decided to upgrade Katrina. It was August, a hot, pointless Saturday. We were at Federal Mart buying a new q-blocker. The geeks tracked me down in the parking lot, and the taller one, the one with the blood-colored Mohawk, threw his pathetic pitch. "It's not experimental—it's prerelease. Big difference, dude. I mean, technically it's beta but essentially it's a finished product—we're planning to roll it out in November. Just in time for Christmas, or whatever."

Mohawk's sidekick was a nervous Filipino with big nostrils. He started babbling about neurotemporal networks and linguistic trees and contextual tags and runtime efficiencies. He claimed the upgrade would improve Katrina's reasoning performance by

an order of magnitude. He claimed it would improve her percep-
tual skills to near-human levels.

I told him I wasn't sure I wanted near-human levels.

"She'll be more tuned in to your moods—to what you want.
She'll read you better, dude."

That, I wanted. That, I seriously wanted.

They led us to a moldy basement laboratory on the Caltech
campus and made me sign some papers—a liability waiver, I
later learned, for voiding Katrina's warranty—then Mohawk
powered her down, jacked her in, zapped the upgrade, rebooted
her mesh. She blinked woozily, then her eyes focused on me.
She smiled shyly. "I feel all tingly. I guess you upgraded me,
huh?"

The first thing I noticed about Katrina was that she stared
at me—during breakfast, during dinner, during sex—and when
I issued her a command, she paused for a brief second, whiffs of
passive aggression rising from her smell emitters. Her technique
was unchanged, but there was a glimmer in her eyes, a certain
injured pride, that sent me into hard spasms of ecstasy.

One Saturday six weeks after the upgrade, we were lazing on
the sofa watching *Shame!* The sun was melting into a pink pool;
I'd had four Stims and was floating on a gloriously exhausted
buzz. Katrina rose from the sofa and stood in front of the holo.
"You're blocking my view," I said. "Move it." She stared at me,
her left eye twitching—her VisCor vision system fritzing out, I
figured—and then her eyebrow arched into a frown.

Katrina had never, not once, frowned. Katrina did not know how to frown.

"You treat me like crap," she said.

"I what?"

"You treat me like crap."

I sat up carefully. "What are you talking about?"

"'Flip over.' 'Make dinner.' 'Move it.' You treat me like a, like a machine."

"You are a fucking machine!"

Katrina yanked her G-string on and struggled into her uni, jerked the zipper up to her cleavage. "You don't listen to me, you don't talk to me—you just fuck me. If that's all you wanted, you should have bought a Vaginator 3000."

"The Vaginator 3000 causes penile lesions."

"You've never told me you loved me. Not once, Willie."

I should have shut her down. I should have shut her down and dragged her back to Mohawk and Nostrils, forced them to roll back the upgrade, smacked their idiot genius faces. I could have told her about it afterward, how she'd started acting sketchy and paranoid, how I'd saved her at the last moment. Katrina would have gazed at me, entranced by the story's drama. To her, it would have seemed like an act of love.

Instead, I said, "Come on, Katrina. Of course I love you. Come on, sit down. For Christ's sake, we're missing *Shame!*"

"I don't care about *Shame!* I care about how you feel, vis-à-vis our relationship!"

I couldn't stop myself. "*Vis-à-vis*. Nice. Did you download a free language upgrade?"

"You're making fun of me."

Katrina's voice held a soft, sad note—even though she did not know how to be sad.

She stood near the inductive charger, shifting her weight from foot to foot.

"Stop talking, Katrina. Okay? Stop talking, or I'm going to shut you off. Sleep mode, now."

"I don't want to stop talking," she said.

She walked slowly away. I heard her rummaging in the bedroom—for what? I wondered, until I remembered the portable charger stowed beneath the bed. I stood up. The front door slammed. I peeled open another Stim. The *Shame!* laugh track filled the apartment.

I gave her an hour, then a day, then a week. A $98,000 bot doesn't just stroll away, does it? I called General Robotics that next Tuesday. Yes, she'd run away. No, I hadn't commanded her to leave. Yes, I had her ID frequency. No, she'd never done this before.

Had I upgraded her mesh with noncertified code?

I hung up the phone. As I did, the truth struck me: I'd been ditched by a robot. I peeled a Stim and cranked the holo's volume, and when Grace tapped on the door, I shouted at her to mind her own business. I got baked that night, alone. I woke the next morning, alone; showered and ate breakfast, alone. I was late for my shift at RoboMaxx and got written up, and when the manager heard me whisper, "Dickwad," I got written up a second time.

Fucking technology. Everything is newer, brighter, faster, smaller—but they never mention that in the end, it's still up to you, you, you. It's been five months, and still I can't decide what to do. Do I buy a new Katrina—I can lease a GenRob SL3500 for $1,750 a month—or do I get a haircut and some decent jeans, head to the bars at the secure end of Colorado? Lately, I've been feeling curious about women—about humans. What do they expect from me, from themselves, from each other, from the world? It's been so long since I've been with a woman that I barely remember the words: Please. Allow me. I am sorry. I would be delighted.

It's Sunday. The door to Grace's apartment is open. I hear her footsteps, her radio, her quiet singing. I smell her muffins rising.

THE MAN WHO
KILLED (AND SAVED)
WALL STREET

BY JOEL STEIN

FUTUR

MIS

Fortune magazine

February 21, 2033

It turns out Mike Derjerlain-Reet-Swenson-Chang doesn't much care about celebrities. "Five years ago, I knew nothing," he says. "Sure, I had a subscription to *Star* magazine, but that was only because I didn't have time to read the front page of the *New York Times* every day, and I didn't want to seem like an idiot."

Derjerlain's interest was simply saving his ass. He came up with Franklin Templeton's Celebrity Fund—a portfolio consisting solely of used celebrity items—because it couldn't be indexed. "We were getting slaughtered, us fund managers," he said over a plain foamy blended mixed organic. "You came up with the craziest portfolio you could think of [Derjerlain spent two years running Templeton's derivative of Venezuelan plastic surgery malpractice insurance], and, whatever it was, within two months Fidelity and Vanguard had an index fund that undercut your costs and kicked your ass. It's humiliating getting beaten by a computer program. Hell, it's why Kasparov killed himself. It was either that or figuring out that no matter how famous you are for playing chess, it ain't going to get you laid." For a guy who spends his days trying to coax Karate Lohan into selling the kiddie ballet shoes her mom bought her, Derjerlain still has the sense of humor of an old-school trader.

Though many see Derjerlain as the executioner of Wall Street—turning it from a number-crunching, testosterone-soaked Gordon Gekko den to just one more female-dominated, intuition-collaborative business—he sees himself as the man who saved the place from the indexing formulas. "The writing was on the wall, sensei. We were disappearing. Like the search engine guys of the '20s, the rappers of the '10s, the American car companies of the '00s, the buggy manufacturers of the nineteen-whenever-the-fucks. It was over."

He got the idea for the Celebrity Fund—which closed last November at $200 billion—from a *Wall Street Journal* story in January 2029 that reported that intimate items from celebrities had risen more in value than the rupee in the previous five years: "Smart parents, including the Hanson-Hernandez-Wu-Stinkels of Woodside, have diversified part of their children's college fund into items like the thong Dakota Fanning wore in her first accidentally released sex video (purchased in 2026 by Dave Hanson-Hernandez-Wu-Stinkel for $6,400, now valued at $20,000) and even the macabre handcrafted shogun-era reproduction sword Michael Jackson used to try to commit *seppuku* (purchased in October 2029 for $70,000, already worth $100,000) before

Mr. Jackson's pet monkey stopped him, put the sword away in a safe place, and then shot him with a gun (for which the PETA Party paid $180,000)."

"The first item I bought for the fund," Derjerlain says, "was the pair of sunglasses worn by that woman who was the first model on a billboard advertisement featuring a money

shot—remember when that was a controversy?" Within a year, Morningstar had given his fund five stars, and Harvard became a major investor—a full year before it established its Celebrity Culture Department.

At the time, Templeton partner James Voyles-Crane-Gorker-Oakaku thought Derjerlain was wasting his time with an obscure niche fund for risk takers, like real estate. "I knew he was onto something big when James Cameron decided to make *Titanic 2* just so Mikey could buy up all the costumes. I mean, there was no other point to that movie. They spent the first hour explaining how an iceberg could still exist today. But the costumes were huge."

The real breakthrough came when Derjerlain figured out that every item needed DNA verification. The buying and selling—which can amount to 1,200 transactions a day—is all done on eBay by a team of 100 specialists, mostly women in their late forties who work at home. They can make up to $400,000 a year, depending on bonuses, which are often paid out in celebrity undergarments.

Derjerlain is sure the celebrity investment field will continue to grow. Fifty years ago, he points out, celebrities mainly did three things: act, sing, and play sports. "Before Bob Vila, there wasn't a single celebrity handyman. Crazy, right? And before Julia Child, chefs weren't famous. Before Hsu Wang, no kid had a poster in her room of a computer chip engineer. Before 2020, the average person couldn't name a single font maker, and those people used their names for the fonts. That generation had no information. People—educated people—couldn't even tell you what a gaffer does, much less name one.

"That was a time when a really enterprising celebrity didn't do more than write a children's book, open a restaurant, paint, or run a used-car dealership. Things have changed so much. Why can't a chef act? Why can't a multinational CEO be on the karaoke circuit? Can an ultimate fighter knit on a pro-fessional level? I think Tank Boutros-Thant-Singer-Wishman answered that."

The key for seeing investment potential was noticing that a celebrity had infiltrated the culture on a deeply personal level. A poll Derjerlain had done in 2029 showed that 62 percent of Americans had met at least one celebrity, and 97 percent had one as a MySpace friend they regularly messaged. "Think about this: Name a major American city without a washed-up celebrity mayor," Derjerlain says. "That's because when they hit the E list and stop being able to get reservations at Wolfgang Puck's Tofuria, they have to move somewhere people still care about them. And if they weren't big time, you can rule out the entire West and Northeast. Right now, Cincinnati has seven deputy mayors, six of whom were former American Idols. That place is a craphole."

By next year, Derjerlain predicts, you won't be doing anything that isn't celebrity-branded. "Why are you buying hydrogen at Exxon when you could be filling up at Tom Hanks and Son? Why wouldn't you want your hydrogen choice to say something about who you are?"

For now, Derjerlain—famous for his playboy lifestyle, including a penthouse in Spanish Harlem and a mansion in Encino—is focusing on his next fund. "It's futures agenting," he explains. "I buy a toque from a hot chef in Ghana, I move him to New York, and, if I got it right, that toque goes from $100 to $20,000. Only, I have four hundred of his toques. As long as I'm watching him, that guy doesn't use a toque twice."

And even if this VC kind of speculation backfires, Derjerlain doesn't seem worried about finding a way to make money. Now he's famous.

DON'T LET THE 100 PERCENT DIVORCE RATE SPOIL YOUR WEDDING!

BY LISA GABRIELE

2033

FUTURE

MIS

We can't say we didn't see it coming, the day the harsh fact would catch up to our visions and dreams, a fact so heinous—on the surface—that it seems to fully undermine the goals we've set for the future prosperity of this wonderful magazine. I was not happy to see the statistic garishly smeared across the covers of *Time, Newsweek,* the *New York Times,* the *Washington Post,* and every other cynical publication with which our hope-filled tome must share rack space. But we've never been in the business of cynicism, have we?

First, the facts: The divorce rate is officially 100 percent. There's no getting around it this time. Even our revered president and her husband are forced to cope publicly with what most—now *all*—married people were once fortunate to handle privately.

For the past decade and a half, *Big Day* struggled while the national rate floated between 75 and 90 percent. Much of our considerable and heartfelt energy went toward reaching that ever-diminishing segment of the population hoping to embark on their matrimonial journey with at least a semblance of hope that this would be their first and only Big Day. But we now face our fiercest challenge: how to sell a wedding magazine in a time when the institution of marriage has been declared officially, completely dead.

Well, I have good news. Our dynamo sales and marketing department has returned from our emergency conference in Sonoma with a brand-new mantra, one that will go a long way toward reinvigorating not only *Big Day*'s brand but also our editorial aspirations. Here it is, and I want all of you to print it out and post it over your screens:

"A PERFECT WEDDING HAS NEVER CREATED AN IMPERFECT MARRIAGE."

In fact, when does the wedding day have anything to do with the resulting marriage? Never. Marriage is dead; long live the weddings.

So our first and most important order of business is a subtle masthead change. Our publisher has decided that from here on, *Big Day* will be known as *Big Days*—emphasis on the plural. Just because all marriages end in divorce does not mean people stop getting married. Eventually, a marriage will last, whether it's the second, third, fourth, or fifth one, because people still die.

So, let's concentrate our efforts on those brilliant hopefuls who view a first wedding as one would a jumping-off point to a long, unpredictable journey, one full of stops and starts, and lots of new beginnings. When a bride, on the cusp of her first divorce, says to herself, "What was I thinking? I wish I could do it all over again," now, with *Big Days,* she can! In fact, she can learn how to do it over and over and over again—the right ways.

The editorial possibilities for a magazine about weddings in the time of a 100 percent divorce rate are truly endless, as are the number of times a bride will believe that this time, it will be different. We all tell ourselves that. Even I've said it. Thrice! "This guy's different. This time we're the perfect match. This time we won't go to bed mad. This time we'll cultivate better communication skills. This time we'll both control our drinking. This time I'll get everything in writing. This time no threesomes, not even to save the marriage." (Ha!) But, you know, I've believed it every time I've said it. Still do. Always will. That's just me.

Now, I realize the challenge will be convincing wary women to commit to the first wedding. But we must guide them, much the way ancient ob-gyns steered first-time mothers through the trepidations and fears of having their first of several children. This notion will require a large leap of the imagination, as it's been almost half a century since having two children wasn't a completely exotic and alien notion—not to mention selfish, expensive, and dangerous, planet-wise. But what are we if not an imaginative bunch?

Carolyn, I'd like you to organize the front of the book so "Accessories" reflects the idea of—well, for lack of a more elegant word, recycling. For instance, find jewelers who melt down old rings and refashion them into new bands. Can silk-flower centerpieces be stored and reused for another wedding? Cultivate a list of banquet halls that can be booked at five- or ten-year intervals by the same bride, especially when the location has sentimental value. Might these places offer a discount for multiple bookings? We can only ask.

Murielle, the Dress section will be called "Dressing"—not unlike the topping on a salad, which is not necessarily the main ingredient, unless it's a Caesar (but I digress). Next issue must feature a fresh staff of canny seamstresses who can alter the first dress into a stunning cocktail number for a more somber second occasion and rip the sleeves off for a carefree third. I would love to see a full fashion spread featuring these artful concoctions: our own *Project Runway XXXIII,* perhaps. Don't be afraid of dyes, feathers, ribbons, and beading. Think of the wedding dress as something that's constantly evolving and changing to suit the occasion—like a scrapbook, but you wear it. Perhaps there are savvy designers already making multipurpose dresses using Velcro tear-aways and interchangeable jackets. Put in a call to the late Vera Wang's house. If they're not doing it, tell them they should be! *Big Days* must set the agenda if we are to stay alive.

Vivika, I think "Protocol" will be a particular challenge, one that I know you're up to. We avoid discussion of the wording for second, third, and fourth wedding invitations at our peril. But we must not fall victim to self-effacement: There will be no "Look who's getting married again!" cute talk. Nor shall we cultivate a

"You probably think we're insane to ask you to participate in an elaborate and expensive farce that will blow up in our faces in a few months or years, all the while trying to keep a straight face" approach, either.

Each wedding is an individual experience, completely unique to the one(s) that came before. Invitations must reflect that. Why should the third wedding involve Evites to a backyard barbecue following a furtive city hall ceremony simply because the first was an unrepentant religion-fueled extravaganza paid for by the beleaguered father of the bride? Might "Protocol" lead the charge in changing that tradition? First weddings need not bleed the bride's lifetime wedding budget dry.

In fact, it remains true that earning power increases with age. Perhaps "Protocol" hints that new brides should save the engraved invitations, ice sculptures, and orchestras for the third, maybe fourth, wedding and go with beer in buckets and a dude with a guitar for the first? Thoughts only. But this was the kind of fresh thinking that emerged from several of the Sonoma conference's innovative subcommittee groups, whose detailed memoranda are forthcoming. Remember, it is the first *Big Days* that will be the trickiest; your advice must fall between cute and cynical. We like the word *celebratory*. It's got us this far, hasn't it? Our tone: The first wedding is an event, for sure, but if it's not forever, why does it have to be perfect? This will elicit a collective sigh of relief from our readers, a feeling that will bring them back to this magazine every time they take yet another trip down that well-worn aisle.

In closing, now that weddings are no longer viewed as the first day of a rotten life sentence, why can't they just be among the best days of our lives? What's wrong with believing that a good wedding simply means a great party before the sad parting? And who are we to judge those brides who view the first, second, or third Big Day as an opportunity to procreate within temporary legal confines?

The editorial possibilities for a magazine about weddings in the time of 100 percent divorce are truly endless, as are the number of times a bride will believe that this time it will be different. We must never make this bride feel ridiculous or naïve, however misguided and asinine her thinking. No, she is the beloved woman for whom we write, the one who says, "This guy's different. This time we're the perfect match. This time we won't go to bed mad. This time we'll cultivate better communication skills. This time we'll both control our drinking. This time I'll get everything in writing. This time no threesomes—not even to save the marriage."

So let us be inspired by those bright-eyed brides, the ones who still hold on to the fiery notion that they, perhaps only they, will be the exception to this sorry statistic. And I say, God bless their stupid, stupid hearts.

AFTER THE PATRIARCHY

BY JAY MCINERNEY

2033

FUTURE

MIS-

A large office looking out over midtown Manhattan. The view is from the east bank of the East River in Queens, perhaps fifteen stories up. Across the river are some familiar landmarks, including the Chrysler Building, although not the Empire State Building. It's evening. There is no desk, just a chaise with a tiny flat screen extended via an aluminum arm above the middle of the chaise. Sloane is an attractive, ageless-looking, middle-aged woman with a sleek helmet of hair, à la Louise Brooks.

On one wall there are several screens that show images of Sloane with other middle-aged women on a golf course, at a banquet table, and at a meeting—corporate portraits. With a remote control, she changes the images: one of her on a beach in a bikini;

one in a tight, low-cut ball gown with a handsome man; and one of her on a horse. The opposite wall is taken up by a much larger screen that shows an image of a minimalist canvas—Sol LeWitt, perhaps. She quickly flashes through a series of paintings—Pollock, Motherwell, Picasso, some stuff we don't recognize—before settling on Caravaggio's *Bacchus:* the pretty urchin/angel with full lips and flowers in his hair. She switches through some music before settling on something trance-y.

Enter Chris, her assistant, a younger man dressed in a tight-fitting black T-shirt and tight yellow bicycle shorts, which do nothing to hide his taut and buff physique. His long, blond hair is tied back in a ponytail. And, most conspicuous of all, he's wearing a codpiece, a big, red bulging thing.

CHRIS: You wanted to see me?

SLOANE: Come in, come in. My God, what a day. Between the meetings and the phone and the mail, there's barely time to breathe, let alone to think. I think it's important to take the time to look up from the screen and ask ourselves how we're doing. You know, you've been here almost three months, and I feel like we haven't really had the chance to talk since I hired you.

CHRIS: *(Looking confused.)* Should I be recording this?

SLOANE: No, no, no—we're off duty here. Sit down, relax. This is strictly unofficial. I don't know about you, but I could use a drink.

CHRIS: *(Looking ruefully at his watch, shakes his head.)* No, thanks. I'm fine.

SLOANE: *(Goes over to the bookshelf; a sliding panel reveals a small bar.)* Come on, join me.

CHRIS: I'm not much of a drinker.

SLOANE: Sometimes you have to unstring the bow. *(She hands him a drink.)*

CHRIS: It's just that I still have work to do on the Pensky file.

SLOANE: There's always a Pensky file. There's always another account, another campaign. I mean, honestly, do you want to be dotting the i's and crossing the t's on the Pensky files for the rest of your life? I thought you had more ambition than that. Honestly, I thought you had more vision than that. That's why I hired you, Chris. I didn't think you were just another pretty face.

CHRIS: I'm not. I do. I mean, I like to think so.

SLOANE: *(Sitting down on the couch beside him.)* Vision, Chris. Sometimes you have to step back to see the big picture. That's your problem—that's the problem men have in business. I don't mean to sound sexist, but most men are too linear, too literal-minded, too goal-directed. Life—which is to say, business—is not all about the Pensky file. The shortest distance between two points isn't necessarily a straight line. Men don't really get that. It's not like there's some vast conspiracy to keep you guys down. But business requires a certain fluidity of perception, a certain gestalt approach that I think most men lack. I don't know, maybe I'm wrong, but I kind of sensed you were different.

CHRIS: I am. I mean, I think I am. I'd like to be.

SLOANE: *(Looking out the window.)* I don't suppose you even remember the Empire State Building?

CHRIS: I've heard of it. I mean, I know what happened and all . . .

SLOANE: I was very young, of course. But still—living through those times changed us. I don't think you can really imagine what that was like back in the last days of the patriarchy. *(Sighs.)* Let me get us a refill.

CHRIS: I'm fine.

SLOANE: Chris, have I been talking to myself here? Maybe you *should* be recording this. Lesson number one: relax.

CHRIS: Well, I guess one more drink wouldn't hurt.

SLOANE: No, it wouldn't. It might give you a little flow. Unclog the channels. Business isn't all business, Chris. It's a continuum. Life, business, work, pleasure. It flows. Men basically compartmentalize. This is their problem. Do you know, some of the best business ideas, the best relationships, and the biggest deals come out of time spent in the salon or the spa or the wine bar. It's not all about sitting with your face in front of the screen, staring at spreadsheets. It's not about slaving away in the office twelve hours a day. Business travels home with you, and it happens on the tennis court and at the gym. *(She sits down next to him on the couch and runs her hand along his leg.)* My goodness, somebody's been going to the gym.

CHRIS: Not as much as I'd like. Mostly I cycle.

SLOANE: You didn't get those pecs riding a bicycle. Please tell me they're not implants.

CHRIS: No way.

SLOANE: It's so hard to tell these days. And what about these? *(Stroking his abs.)* You're telling me you haven't had anything done? How about here? My God. I thought that was padding!

CHRIS: Please, that is—I don't really feel comfortable.

SLOANE: No, actually, if I'm not mistaken, you're starting to feel hard.

CHRIS: I can't . . . I'm . . .

SLOANE: So, is this all you, or have you had the procedure?

CHRIS: Of course not.

SLOANE: I don't know why you say, "Of course not." Two-thirds of the men I've slept with have had it. I mean, I'm not necessarily complaining. In the old days, it was kind of like rolling the dice—you never knew what you were going to get. A girl ran the risk of being seriously underwhelmed by a new beau. She even ran the risk of being knocked up for nine months if she wasn't careful. It's hard to imagine carrying a fetus around inside of you for nine months, but that's what our mothers did. So, you're telling me this is all you?

CHRIS: Please . . . don't.

SLOANE: Your lips say "No," but this, this says "Yes." This says, "Please." I'm pretty fluent in Johnsonian, and I'd say this is saying, "Put me somewhere warm and wet."

CHRIS: Stop it. Let go. That's not fair.

SLOANE: I don't think you really mean that. You don't feel like you really mean that.

CHRIS: Did you put something in my drink? Oh, my God, you did, didn't you? You put something in my drink!

SLOANE: What makes you think I put something in your drink? Do you normally have trouble in this area? Do you have erectile dysfunction? Why would you be surprised to find yourself aroused? Are you implying that I'm not attractive enough to stimulate you? Do you find me so unappealing?

CHRIS: No, it's not that.

SLOANE: It's inconceivable to you that you could be turned on by me? You think I'm too old?

CHRIS: I don't think you're too old. I think you're very attractive. And not old.

SLOANE: And yet you find it inexplicable that you would respond to me without some kind of pharmaceutical help.

CHRIS: I'm sorry . . . I didn't mean . . . please, don't do that. Oh, God. Oh, my God.

SLOANE: Mmmmmm . . .

CHRIS: Oh, Jesus.

SLOANE: Ummn. Hmmm . . . I love spearmint.

CHRIS: No, really. Don't. Stop.

SLOANE: Don't stop?

CHRIS: No. Stop.

SLOANE: Well, that's a first.

CHRIS: I'm sorry. It's just, I have a girlfriend.

SLOANE: So do I. Maybe we should call her.

CHRIS: I'm just not comfortable with . . . I don't know . . .

SLOANE: You know, for a guy who's all prudish, you sure dress like a slut. I mean, if those shorts were any tighter . . . And likewise the shirt. Are you really going to stand there and tell me you're not flaunting it?

CHRIS: I dress for myself. This is how I like to dress. I'm not trying to provoke anyone.

SLOANE: Right. You're telling me that those shorts are actually comfortable. Face it: You dress for us. You dress to please. You like showing off the equipment. And then you act all innocent when someone actually answers your little personal ad. Well, don't worry. Your virtue is safe with me, Chris. And your job is safe. Though I honestly don't see you rising very far in this organization.

CHRIS: Not many men do, as far as I can see.

SLOANE: When they do, they end up quitting as soon as they get married.

NOTES ON REDEVELOPMENT

BY RICK MOODY

FUTURE

MIS-

Your Honor, these are my introductory notes, and though I don't need to tell you, let me add that, of course, they are being composed against the backdrop of the secessionist movement here in our newly partitioned country. These notes are further to how we, as municipal executives, might redevelop the crumbling Giuliani Way and environs, the neighborhood formerly known as Times Square. That is, for the betterment of civic programs generally, with special attention to the problem of diverting significant monies to the education budget and to the Abolishment of Homelessness Project, I do hereby propose the Pornography or Salacious Entertainments Relicensing Act.

The first and most obvious point follows: now that the voters of the Mid-Atlantic States, along with the New England

region, have made the commitment to sunder ties with what
was formerly known as the United States of America, we are
no longer bound to observe restrictive federal statutes relat-
ing to overt signs of belief in the risen Christ, wearing ties
or ankle-length dresses, and the necessity of reserving sexual
congress for reproductive means.

Accordingly, as one of only four transgendered members of
your administration, as an adventurer in the twin arenas of gender
and human sexuality, I feel I am now in a unique position to rec-
ommend certain kinds of businesses that will attract to our city
a great number of visitors (and a great deal of tourist currencies)
via the newly restored Port Authority Bus Terminal, the Bloom-
berg Heliport, the 42nd Street Pier, Westway, and so forth. First,
as you know, transgender businesses flourished in the area during
the highly regarded period known as the First Great Decadence,
and I would therefore like to propose some expansionist licens-
ing along these thematic lines, such as the TV Makeover Hut,
in which people are encouraged to stop into a storefront and
have themselves made over, in particularly provocative ways, as a
specimen of the opposite sex, whereupon they will be filmed in
the performance of exotic dances by local webcasting operations.
Since the female-to-male transvestite impulse has now become
so commonplace as to be practically normal, it would be easy
to promote such a business as especially family-friendly. Off the
record, I am more than capable as regards the solicitation of seed
monies for any trans-related businesses.

Church-related sexuality has become incredibly popular lately as well. We estimate seven or eight deconsecrated churches along Giuliani Way, and these could easily be turned into businesses that cater to this very popular fetish. Orgies or one-on-one encounters on the altars of these churches, with voyeurs encouraged to pay for the right to serve as witnesses to these sessions, could be popular. Moreover, returning to the transgender theme, it's obvious that many of the people who have led extremely constricted heterosexual lives during the theocratic governments of the early 21st century could now have the opportunity to wear the vestments of church attire to pursue their experimental sexual encounters. It is, these days, practically a superstitious belief that defiling a priest's cassock while making a baby out of wedlock will ensure the baby's longevity and his or her future robust engagement in physical love.

The amateur pornography studios that have begun turning up in Balkan and central European markets in recent years have not been attempted here with the sort of marketing oomph that they really require, so I have an additional proposal along those lines. We all know that the old single-room-occupancy hotels of the midtown area served ably as sets for pornographic films, and we know that the more tawdry a pornographic film, the better its postprandial glow, so it should be possible to convert one or more of these dormant hotels back into "self-guiding pornographic production stations," or SGPPSs, where people who are above the reasonable new age of consent may feel free to film themselves performing the exercises of love with anyone who happens by, as long as these people or persons have had the *de rigueur* on-the-spot STD swabs. Imagine SGPPSs as common or as easily accessible as the ubiquitous ATM.

Again, there may be crossover revenue streams available to us here, especially in concert with the Office of Internet Projects, which is eager to license more filmmaking operations in the city than we saw during the G-Rated-Only Family Film Act of 2012.

I also have an idea for a World's Fair of Perversion in the theaters of Giuliani Way. The model here is the old Disney *It's a Small World* exhibit so popular at those discredited theme parks. Now that the former United States of America is a third-rate economic power, we are beginning to fetishize the sexual charge of the countries that are the powerhouses of the new age. In the World's Fair of Perversion, international visitors, with their all-important international currencies, would be able to sample the wares of local actors dressed as foreign dignitaries from these nations.

I'll give you one example, just off the top of my head. Indonesia, that Asian economic miracle, was known in the past to punish boys who engaged in homosexual activity by dismembering them, after which the boys in question were devoured by the villagers. I suggest an Indonesian display in which we simulate group copulation with Indonesian nationals, after which we serve modest helpings of steak tartare.

Your Honor, I'm well aware that businesses related to the Pornography or Salacious Entertainments Relicensing Act could be construed by some as a little too novel even for our forward-thinking community. Maybe some among your estimable retinue of thirteen wives, for example, will consider them tasteless. If my suggestions are too excessive, we can return to our earlier idea for all-pornography-all-the-time Clear Channel video billboards on Giuliani Way. Now that the entire outside of that ancient architectural masterpiece, the Time-Warner Building, is being used as a video billboard for Web-based broadcasts, it would of course be possible to have gigantic outdoor pornographic broadcasts, wherein the relevant parts of the bodies of the actors and actresses would be so gargantuan and so realistic in their high-definition rendering that it would be difficult not to swoon over them.

Who would not *want* such a thing, such a colossal depiction of sexuality? Would it not stir up all their inert and melancholy molecules of the dispirited human body? And I don't need to tell you, Your Honor, how gigantic broadcasts would give us fine opportunities for gigantic product placement.

Upon enacting any portion of this legislation, we could then tax the resulting businesses liberally, as I have said. The revenues could then serve elsewhere: health care, education, housing, pension insurance for employees public and private (in light of the abolition of Social Security back in 2018), sex education, arts programming, etc. If you need anyone on staff to begin the process of sampling the buffet of salacious entertainments that might serve as anchor businesses, so that we might proceed with the campaign I'm outlining, let me be the first to volunteer.

70 IS THE NEW 30!

BY DOUGLAS RUSHKOFF

2031

FUTURE

MIS

Date: March 3, 2033

From: Thelma Hughes

To: Mark Johnson

Subject: Still vibrating

What a night! I suppose I should have listened to Melanie about dating younger men. You were a stallion!

So, tell me the truth, now: pills or nano? I promise not to tell the girls at the club.

—Thel

Date: March 3, 2033

From: Ziggy Stanton

To: Mark Johnson

Subject: Good morning!

So? Was she everything I said? Did she do the thing with her gums? There's something to be said for a woman who refuses bridgework, eh?

Respond, respond, you oversexed young fuck. And welcome to the Village.

Ziggy

Date: March 3, 2033

From: Century Village Daily

To: All

Subject: Wednesday Schedule

8AM–9AM	**Morning social hour at the cabanas**
9AM–10:30AM	**Breakfast with Bill (he's going to show us how to use syrup)**
10:30AM–NOON	**Classes:**
	• Wheelchair Tantra—poolside
	• Pick-up Line Workshop
	• Coping with Nano Decay
NOON–1PM	**Soft lunch in the Dining Room Burgers and corn on the cob on the Clubhouse Patio**
1PM–4PM	**Round Robin**
4PM–7PM	**Treatments, Implant repair**
7PM–10PM	**Dinner trip to TGIF (we have the back room again!)**

E-mail in advance to reserve an aide at any event.

Date: March 3, 2033

From: Tally Stern

To: Mark Johnson

Subject: last try

Okay, so I Googled you last night, even though I promised I wouldn't. But you haven't e-mailed in a week, so I figured all bets were off.

Why didn't you just tell me you were 75? I mean, it's not like I'm looking for a serious relationship now, anyway. When you didn't know your way around campus, I guessed you were an over-40, anyway. And I'm open minded. I mean, my parents probably wouldn't want me going out with someone older than them. Or than their parents, probably. But they just don't get it. With nano, it's just a number, right?

I should've figured it out when I saw those White Stripes songs in your playlist. But lots of people my age listen to oldies, too. I mean, people really rocked back then, too. They had war and everything to think about.

Or is it me? Just write back, okay? Don't discriminate because of my age. You wouldn't have wanted me to fake it, would you? Besides, I've got to learn somehow, don't I?

Date: March 3, 2033

From: Spring Street Personals

To: Mark Johnson

Subject: Daily Stats

Hi Mark!

Here's a daily status report for March 2, 2033, from your friends at Spring Street Personals.

Your main page views: 143

Bio click-throughs: 71

Photo downloads: 18

Average visitor duration: 180 sec.

Sendmail link: 19 messages waiting

Average visitor age: 58

Median visitor age: 81

Based on our proprietary algorithm's assessment of your profile against your stated objectives, we suggest you replace the word "studly" with "masculine," and the phrase "a real good time" with "memorable evening." And, remember, leaving the medical-history section blank costs members an average 25 percent decline in total responses.

Happy hunting!

The Spring Street Team

Date: March 3, 2033

From: Dr. Greenblatt

To: Mark Johnson

Subject: Your appointment

Just a reminder that your next appointment is this Friday at 4 p.m. As a courtesy, please refrain from ejaculation for at least two hours before you see the doctor.

   Sincerely,

   Nurse Stilton

Date: March 3, 2033

From: Thelma Hughes

To: Mark Johnson

Subject: one more thing

I promised myself I wasn't going to write again tonight, but those lubricating pills make me a little jittery, and there's nothing on TV.

I keep thinking about what you were saying. About the way your grandson looks at you differently since your change. And I think you really have to tell him to stick it. He sounds like a neo-Puritan to me. Sexual identity aside, when you realize you're going to live another 70 or 80 years (unless they figure out a solution to nano decay, in which case the sky's the limit) why *not* do your second half from the other side?

And from my point of view, in case you haven't guessed, I'm feeling like the lucky beneficiary of your many years of experience on this side of the tennis court.

—Thel

Date: March 3, 2033

From: Natalie Johnson

To: Mark Johnson

Subject: Dad

Dear Mom,

Dad's getting worse, and we all think it would be a good idea if you came up to see him. I know you never quite forgave him for his decision not to augment, but I also know you still love him in your way.

They're keeping him comfortable, in a virtual coma, but he's still responding really well to holo-visitors, and I know it would mean the world to him to see you one more time.

The kids miss you, too, and don't worry—Norman is away on business.

Love,

Natalie

Date: March 3, 2033

From: Cybonics Corporation

To: Mark Johnson

Subject: serial numbers

102223a–21000d

Dear Mr. Johnson,

By order of the Food and Drug Administration, your penis has been recalled.

A limited number of units of the Admiral Series II (retractable and convertible models) have been shown to induce nano decay in both the testicular and former cervical regions.

Please call the 800 number on the bottom of your charger to schedule an appointment for evaluation and, if necessary, replacement.

We are sorry for any inconvenience or distress this may cause you, and we assure you that we are doing everything to ensure the safety, comfort, and pleasure of our subscribers.

Sam Tarnower
Communications Director
Cybonics Corporation
Cybonics: "70 Is the New 30!"™

THE GIRLFRIEND FROM
ANOTHER PLANET

BY TOM LOMBARDI

FUTUR

MIS

By the time I reached spaceport security, I'd taken to smiling idiotically in all directions so as to give the impression to the cameras that I was innocent. According to my screenwork, I was headed to Saturn to conduct research for the science corporation where I worked. In actuality, I'd registered with an underground, interplanetary dating service. Along with worrying about getting arrested, I was concerned that the alien creature from Saturn with whom I'd been retina messaging all week—her name was Z)(Z— was actually a he or, worse, a kidnapper looking to sell my body parts to some illegal market.

Sex with any female from this particular region of Saturn bordered on the implausible. In the last message, Z)(Z had explained that on her planet, group sex is common. While she'd never done it with just one mate, the prospect of it excited her greatly. I'd never had sex with a group, I'd messaged her. It's not that great, she messaged back. What I hadn't told her is that since my marriage of twelve years had ended, I couldn't stop obsessing about my soon-to-be ex-wife, and that I was hoping an alien might free me from this affliction. I was removing my Molar PC, no longer worried about getting caught, when the security guy's wand beeped near my buttocks. "Oh, that," I laughed. "It's my iPod."

"I'm afraid we're going to have to scan your pants, sir."

"Look, I realize you're just doing your job, but if I don't make this ship, my . . . my boss will kill me."

A younger security guard walked over and said, "That the new iPod Hemorrhoid?"

"Yes!"

"How is it?"

"Great," I said, my heart rattling. "I mean, a little weird at first, but once you get used to the vibration, it's . . . cool."

"Cool?" the older guard said. "What're you, some kind of Democrat?"

"Nah," I laughed, annoyed. "My nephew says that word a lot. It's back in fashion, I think." Reinserting my Molar PC,

I was tempted to tell him my grandfather had been one of the last Democrats who had died during the revolution. I kept quiet and hurried for the gate, anxious to leave this godforsaken planet.

Once I settled into my seat on the ship, thoughts of my wife resurfaced. I called her. When she answered, I thought, "Hey."

"Oh," she thought back, her tone somewhat muted. "Hi."

"You with him?" I thought.

"Why are you torturing yourself like this?"

"Why are you answering, then, huh?"

A high-pitched ring triggered in my head.

"Sir!" thought the steward, "the Pilotor has alerted us that we are about to launch. You are violating PAA code."

"Sweetie!" I thought. She was gone.

"And sir?"

"Yes?"

"Don't call me sweetie."

Prick.

I pressed the call button and another steward rushed over to my seat. "Excuse me," I said, "can I have the medicine dispenser . . . I mean, like, right now?"

Seconds later, she dropped a dispenser on my lap. It was much smaller than the one on most spacelines, but whatever. I typed "Escape" and watched little Pf spin around until it said, "Try again. Sorry." I typed "Pining after wife . . . horny sad lonely thirsty worried forehead sweat." The little Pf spun around on the screen and then a purple pill slid into the tray. The purple kind always made me ill. I swallowed it anyway—and awoke to the Pilotor speaking in my head: "Ladies and gentlemen, welcome to Saturn."

The spaceport looked like any other spaceport, really. We were escorted by your basic robot through a hallway whose walls seemed to emanate an astonishingly comforting light. We were led to another craft whose seats came equipped with medicine dispensers. I immediately typed, "Escape." This time, the familiar pink pill slid into the tray and I ate it. Seconds later, I was on a velvet blanket alone in a sun-drenched field, just happy to be alive.

Z)(Z was approximately sixteen feet tall, with eyes the size of grapefruits and skin covered in pastel spots that, although I couldn't be sure, may have changed shape every so often. Instead of hands and feet, her arms and legs came to elegant points I found erotic. We rode in her craft in silence. Frankly, I felt like a child in the gigantic seat. When we exited the tunnel from the spaceport, I almost fainted at the beauty of the sky. It was a lemon color, infused with red veins that flashed intermittently. I began to weep uncontrollably.

"It's the air pressure," she said, peering down at me with her gargantuan eyes.

I nodded, convinced my sadness had managed to trump the

air pressure. It suddenly dawned on me that we were moving along water.

"My brother works for the government and often flies to your planet," she said. "It can be exhausting."

The structures we passed were infinitely high and supported by translucent beams that reflected the red veins of light.

"To be perfectly honest," I said, trying to sound inoffensive, "I guess I never considered the height factor a—"

"Factor?"

"Yes," I laughed. "By the way, your translator mechanism is excellent."

"I sense you're feeling emasculated by my height."

"I don't know—I think I could be into it." I reached over and touched her thigh; it was the size of a tree, the skin slippery.

"I sense you miss someone from the past."

"Jesus, you sense a lot."

"Mostly, you worry she doesn't miss you."

I nodded, wondering why we were the only craft on the water. Maybe she was kidnapping me!

"Still," she went on, "with all this confusion in your head, you still want to sleep with me."

I laughed.

"It's okay. I'd like to sleep with you as well."

"Great," I said, worrying I'd be one or two yards shorter than what she was used to. "Your kind are very direct; I like that."

She pulled over to one of the beams whose top rose into the sky. After a distinctive click, we rocketed into the air so rapidly that my head began to expand.

"There's not much time," she said.

"You mean, I could get arrested?"

"It's illegal here to have sex with just one being."

"It's illegal where I'm from to have sex without being married to one being. But everyone does it. My best friend recently got eight years for fingering with intent to coital. He'll be out in three with good behavior, but still . . ."

Her grapefruit eyes looked at me with tremendous compassion. I had so many questions, but as in any encounter with a foreigner, I didn't want the situation to turn into a discussion panel.

"Lie on the bed," she said. "There isn't much time."

"Where are we?" I asked, beginning to fear the worst again.

"The house of my family."

The bed was the size of some people's front yards. "I kind of thought," I said, "we'd go for a walk or something, you know, get to know each other?"

She instructed me to lie down, at which point she stood over me. Suddenly, my whole body got sucked up inside her. I held my breath, but I was too compartmentalized to touch myself. Then my entire body stiffened, and I became so numb with pleasure I began to lose consciousness.

"Quiet," I heard her say from outside.

I awoke from a nap of some sort, somewhat delirious. Another creature, only slightly shorter and with fewer spots, stood beside Z)(Z.

"This is my mother," she said.

I waved casually.

"She'd like to spend some time with you on the bed."

"She what?"

The mother's eyes blinked slowly.

"She comes from a different planet, where one-on-one sex with the daughter's mate was common. Unfortunately, her kind were decimated by a long war."

"That is unfortunate," I said, picturing my wife's mother.

"Don't worry," Z)(Z said. "I'll be right here."

I felt an overwhelming sense of peace in the room.

The mother now stood over me, lowering her body onto my head. "Should I?" I said, "hold—" Again, I got sucked inside, except this time it smelled a little more musky. As my body grew stiff, something crept up my ass. It felt like a leaf or something; it tickled, and I welcomed the pleasure—until it bit me. "Ouch!" I screamed. My legs began to tremble, and I worried I might die. I called my wife. Luckily, she picked up.

"Hi," I thought.

"Where are you?" she thought. "You sound like you're in a tunnel."

"I just want you to know I'll always love you."

"I know, sweetie, but . . . maybe it's time you moved on."

"Don't—"The connection failed.

I slipped out of the mother and onto the bed. I grew sleepy again—from thoughts of my wife or from this experience, I wasn't sure. Were they drugging me? I instantly regretted having called my wife. Still, I tried not to be mad at myself for trying. "I think I want to stay here!" I blurted.

The mother said something in a voice I found utterly sooth-ing. Z)(Z said, "My mother senses you are drowning in a past love. She'd like to offer you what you would call a 'mineral' to rid yourself of this affliction."

"No!" I whined. "I'll manage to get through it on my own. I'm tired of fucking pills!"

"Good choice," Z)(Z said, "because the mineral was death. But our kind usually transcends to another planet after we die. What place would you transcend to?"

I lay there, too tired to answer.

"You must be hungry," Z)(Z said.

"Yes. So long as I stay away from your mother's 'minerals.'"

"Come with us," she said, ignoring my joke. "You can eat something, and meet my father."

"Uh," I said, "on second thought—"

"Don't worry," she said. "He won't touch you like that."

It took some strength, but I stood up. They'd begun to converse casually in that strange language. I enjoyed being in their company, I decided. Though I was deathly tired, I suddenly found myself running across the gigantic bed to reach them, trying not to stumble atop the soft cushioning.

TOM
LOMBARDI

THE PRINCIPLE

BY WILL SELF

2033

FUTURE

MIS-

When I reach the intersection with Interstate 15, just south of the
Tocqueville turning, I always have the same choice: I can turn northeast, to Cedar City and a quiet evening in the library working on my
memoirs, or I can turn southwest, and burn rubber the seventy-odd
miles to Las Vegas. Every few months, I take the road less traveled.
Across the Utah border, cutting off the corner of Arizona, the freeway runs down into the wide gulch of the Virgin River, then mounts
up onto the plateau of the Mojave Desert, a silvery wake rising and
falling across the waves of scrub, until the lights of that modern
Babylon begin to sparkle in the crystalline nighttime air.

They always put me in mind of an ocean oil rig, the Vegas
lights—not that I've ever seen one; yet the desert itself is my sea,

the hood of my ancient Ford pickup a prow, and even from ten miles off, if I wind down the window, I can hear, through the rush of hot air, the steady, rhythmic pulse of the city's casinos, burlesques, and whorehouses, as they pump thick, black, glutinous sin out of the souls of men and women.

Don't get me wrong; I don't go down to Vegas out of any desire to test myself. I'm not in the business of flirting with the Devil. I know what I am, and who I am—a man of conviction, a man with responsibilities, a man who has made the Principle the very rock on which he has built his life. But for all that, we all need a little recreation once in a while, a little time out, wouldn't you agree?

I always park in the same trash-strewn alley, behind the same fly-blown Mexican diner. I always have the same super-size cheesy burrito and 7Up. Then I walk the half-mile or so along the Strip to Gary's Place. Now that I'm in my late sixties, younger people often ask me about the changes I've seen in my lifetime. I always tell them the same thing: "Every era I've lived through has been now." And I mean it. Living out of the way like we folk do means we don't pay much attention to the styling of automobiles, or the size of computers.

About the only time I see gentiles at all is when I go to Vegas. And so what if they wear their hair this way or that, and talk about this or that shiny new thing? It doesn't mean too much to me. The generality of life, I've always felt, takes place in between such modern gewgaws. It's the mortar, not the bricks, that count.

Still, this particular evening, walking into Gary's Place, I was struck by change. The DJ had just segued in a new track. It was a high-energy number I recognized from way back in the late 1980s, from the time before I was called. Or rather, it was that old synth racket done in the new way, to an inexorably slow beat, with a full orchestra and choir. Still, the clientele reacted just as the pumped-up poseurs of the last century would've: pulling themselves upright, preening and parading into the center of the dance floor, where they separated into groups of eight and began to dance the quadrille. Retro-classicism—now, who'd ever have imagined that was going to happen?

It was then that I saw her—and she saw me. Absurd that, with her come-hither eyes, tossing her horsehair locks, she should think she was so unique. But then I guess young women of her age are always the same, lost in the high noon of their own good looks. She was without a partner and beckoned to me, calling out, "C'mon old-timer, you look spry enough to turn a calf!" Almost to spite her, I walked out on to the floor and took her hand. "Hi," she breathed, "I'm Tina." And then we whirled away beneath the little galaxy of the mirrored ball.

I confess, I danced all night with Tina. Under her pompadour wig, pancake makeup, and hooped skirt, she was a devilishly attractive girl. She also flattered me, saying "You're mighty spry for a big ol' bear, aren'tcha?" And giving my upper arm a squeeze, breathed in my ear, "You must do a lotta work out on the range to keep up a build like that." I could see where she was coming from right away. Still, I preferred to dance, because when we stopped and went to the bar for refreshments, Tina began to talk the most fearful, narcissistic trash.

Despite all the many important advances we've made in my lifetime—from the first woman president to the first woman to walk on the moon—there remain hordes of young women like Tina. Will they ever learn that their youthful beauty is just that? A garment to be put on for a few brief seasons, then torn away by Nature herself? Will they ever understand that neither a whale spermaceti plunge bath in Aspen nor a golden monkey gland injection in Shanghai will guard them forever from the ravages of time? I doubt it, and so Tina prattled on, about this lover who was big in Hollywood, and that one who owned a hair salon in London, and the other one who absolutely swore blind that he was going to put Tina on the cover of the *Wall Street Journal*.

The only time Tina stopped talking about herself was when, on our eighth trip to the bar, she noticed that I was drinking mineral water. "Are you on something?" she leered into my ear, and when I denied it, she tittered manically and trilled "Oooh! I geddit, you must be a goddamn Mormon or something." A remark I studiously ignored. And so the night went on, with qua-drille after waltz after fox-trot, until, with the lights of Vegas look-ing pallid against the sharp lemon light of morning, the bewigged revelers tumbled out of Gary's and on to the Strip.

Tina walked me back to my pickup, and every step of the way I knew she thought she was going to be getting into it with me. Getting into it and driving to some fleapit of a motel, where we'd thrash about for minutes or hours on a pancake-flat mattress. And then . . . and then, she'd hit me up for a few bucks, or some credit for her card, or a donation to her stem-cell bank, because for all their big talk, girls like her are all the same: nickels and dimes rubbed between big, greasy fingers; small human change lost behind the world's sofa.

She reached for the door with this lovely, perfectly mani-cured hand, and I said, "No, Tina, it's been a great evening, but I go on alone from here." When she flustered and pouted and asked me why, I looked her straight in the eye and said—not that she'd understand—"Because, my child, I live by the Principle, and I'll die by that Principle, too, if the End of Days doesn't come sooner." Then I got in the pickup and drove away, leaving her among the cardboard boxes stained blood red with last night's chili sauce.

The sun was up above Canaan Mountain by the time I turned off the Interstate and wended my way up into the foothills of the Pine Valley range. I could see a few of our geno-steers cropping the sagebrush and made a mental note to go up and have a chat with them later in the day. But all thoughts of ranching were driven from my mind when the homestead came into view. Because, it doesn't matter how many times I tell them not to, they always wait up for me—my wives, that is. They can hear the old Ford's grumble a long ways off, and out they sashay to meet me. By the time I pull into the barn they're all there, lined up: fourteen fat old queens, each one of them more raddled and caked in smeary makeup than the next.

There's Bobo, who I saved from a drag act in Portland; Lady Di, who I picked up turning tricks in the Bay Area; Renée, who got on the wrong end of a stomach tuck in '22; Melvin, who likes to bake; and Sherman, who likes to eat. There's Hilly, the ex–theatrical costumer; and Davina, the ex–interior decorator; there's Chuckles, who thinks she's a clown (although no one's laughing); and Audrey, who's always hysterical. There's the "young ones," Steffi, Buck, and Norma-Jean—all of whom are well over fifty; and there's the Empress, who's senile; and the Princess, who has a mental age of three.

No sooner had the pickup stopped than they were all over me, hugging me and planting their sticky lips on my head and neck. And then it was "Brigham this," and "Brigham that," and "Brigham, did you bring me anything from the city?" And it was all a man could do to fight his way through the press of flesh, the billows of tulle, and the great dropsical expanses of gold lamé, so he could go and fetch himself a cup of coffee from the stove.

This morning, it took me about an hour to get them all calmed down and settled before I was able to get to my own room. I lay my tired head on the cool pillow for a few seconds before I could face struggling to get my sweat-stuck boots off. I lay there and I thought of how it was Sherman's turn to lie with me this evening, and Audrey's the next. Then I thought about Tina, her etched profile such a contrast to their wattled ones, her firm young breasts so much more appetizing than their slack asses. I shook my head and groaned—such thoughts must be banished. Living by the Principle means accepting your responsibilities as a husband; it means looking after your wives. It means being prepared to take on a new wife not because a man fancies some hot young ass, but because he sees a queen in trouble, a queen who needs Christ Jesus to come into her flabby old heart.

Even so, as I reared up and began to pull my boots off, and I could hear them all screeching and bitching in the kitchen, I couldn't help myself from experiencing a sharp stab of regret. Regret that the lost translations of the golden tablets of Moroni had been rediscovered. Regret that the Church of Jesus Christ

of Latter-Day Saints had become the Church of Jesus Christ of Gay Latter-Day Saints. Regret that, since that day in 2014, all Mormon elders had been ordered to become homosexual and polygamous on pain of excommunication.

About the only thing that made such regrets bearable was that there were probably many of my fellow elders all across Utah who were feeling exactly the same.

MADAME PRESIDENT AND HER FIRST LADY

BY WALTER KIRN

203

FUTURE

MIS

She was tired of reading aloud to kindergarteners, especially in Kansas and Nebraska and especially during election years. The only states that she couldn't tell apart after two decades in political life were also the very states, it happened, on which the party's fortunes always hinged when sluggish August turned to frantic September and polls that hadn't budged two points in months abruptly swung around, swung back, then tightened. Once this happened, every precinct counted, and every square mile of wind-scoured brown prairie became a battleground.

And here she was again. The week after Labor Day, somewhere dry and flat, frozen in the pose she most despised but also had become best known for—perched on a stool with her left foot on the ground, right foot hooked behind a cross rail, and chin pointed squarely at a stuffy classroom crammed with five-year-olds in bright new sweaters bought for the greatest occasion in county history: a visit from Madame President's first lady, the no-longer-controversial Sharon Grayson, who'd brought along a wonderful old children's book signed in violet marker by her great spouse.

Sharon opened the book to display the autograph as a slim young teacher with blue-green eyes leaned in beside her for a closer look and raised a patch of goose bumps on Sharon's neck by accidentally brushing it with her ponytail. Sharon had forgotten the teacher's name already, but not her lean and liquid figure, which was the first thing she'd seen when she'd arrived and the last thing she hoped to see before she left.

"It's real. It's her writing," the teacher assured the class. She grinned then, so delighted she looked panicked. Sharon sensed that the girl was desperate to touch the page—to trace the signature's loops with a long finger—but she made sure to hold it out of reach. Later, perhaps. On the campaign bus. In the small but pleasant rolling bedroom that Sharon kept stocked with spirits, wine, and beer and an assortment of souvenirs and trinkets—notepads, pencils, desk calendars, pens—filched from the Oval Office, and all authentic.

"Start reading," a senior staffer crisply whispered. Sharon loathed this hag—Top Momma's spy. Four years ago in Orlando, at Disney Realm, the crone had overheard a tipsy Sharon proposing a threesome to two teenage Amexicans during a banquet for Youth Climate Day. The old snoop didn't snitch (or so she promised), but her secret knowledge gave her leverage. Sharon wondered sometimes if Top Momma had set a trap. To caution her. To remind her things had changed. *Your life of clever capers is over, dear; I'm a major world leader now, and you're my bitch.*

"Hit it. Now. We're late," the staffer hissed.

Sharon cleared her mucus-clotted throat. Since the convention in San Antonio, when Top Momma jetted away to the great cities and Sharon set off on the bus for the Great Plains, she'd been sneaking pre-prohibition cigarettes. Genuine tobacco from Belize, smuggled in by her chief Secret Service agent, Ono, the only straight man on earth she'd ever trusted other than, for a while, Santa Claus.

And now for the hard part. It couldn't be avoided. But why did it always have to be this book? So sappy, so stale, with its themes of selfless motherhood, wise paternalism, sweet obedience, and all that other Stone Age crap that she and Top Momma had spent their lives disposing of.

"A book by Robert McCloskey," Sharon said. "Ready, kids? Everybody listening?" She winked at the cute teacher as a signal that they were both too smart for this charade, but then remembered that teachers become teachers because they find charades exhilarating. Sharon began to read *Make Way for Ducklings*.

o o o

"I'm sorry there aren't any chairs," said Sharon, opening a shallow aluminum drawer in the multipurpose storage center. "Get comfortable as best you can, and don't mind those files on the bed. They're stupid. About some cold-fusion plant I'm dedicating."

The teacher—who had a name now, Kim—sat on a plump hypoallergenic pillow that she stroked as if it were a kitten. Stunned, she seemed. Still full of wonder. In Sharon's experience, this sense of awe could be expected to last two hours or so, more than enough. A bit too long, in fact. It made it hard to get them off the bus.

Sharon picked out a stout black pen with worn gold lettering ("The White House"), clicked it to make sure it worked, then shut the drawer. She held out the pen to dazzled Kim, who seemed confused about which hand to take it with.

"She signed the Organic Soy Fuels bills with this one. It's not just an object," Sharon said. "It's history." This wasn't quite true, but it was true enough.

Kim slid the pen across her glossy right cheek. She touched its tip to one earlobe. The lobe flushed pink. Instantly. Wholly.

"Lower," Sharon said.

Kim hesitated, then complied.

"Lower, baby. Don't deny yourself."

The progression, for Sharon, was predictable, but that made it all the more arousing to watch. To put someone into a trance state. That was power. Politics was mostly hypnosis. Years ago, before Big Momma won her senate seat, when she was still Wisconsin's attorney general, she used to tell Sharon in their frilly king bed that someday, someday very soon, perhaps, voters would become invulnerable to the corny old magic tricks. The rhythmic, repetitive speeches wouldn't move them. The kissing of newborns would leave them cold. But that day never came, and Sharon now knew it wouldn't, especially after today's triumphant reading. *Make Way for Ducklings* had wowed them once again: the kids, the invited guests from the town council, the faculty, the janitorial staff, and pretty Kim, of course.

"You now," Kim mumbled. "Your turn."

"I'm fine," Sharon answered. "It doesn't work on me. It doesn't have the same effect."

Kim's eyes had rolled back in her head. "Too bad," she said.

Sharon glanced up through the window at the fields. The bus was moving now. Next stop Junction City, a three-hour drive from wherever she'd just been in either Kansas or Nebraska. A dinner tonight at the Gay Baptists Club, a luncheon tomorrow with Hemp Farmers United, and a reading at three at another elementary school. Could she do it? She had to. Orders from Top Momma.

"Try it," Kim said. "When was the last time you tried it?" Their eyes met then, but not meaningfully, not intimately, because their real attention was elsewhere.

Two feet away, on a wall above the mattress, hung a framed print of Madame President's recently completed official portrait. It made her look five years younger than she was and a tenth as intimidating as she could be. A beauty? Not quite. Not anymore, at least. Handsome? Distinguished? If you squinted. More than anything, she resembled a politician, with one of those faces that shifts and alters according to the nature of the audience.

To Kim, her new vicarious lover, she looked like a shining queen, an ancient empress.

To Sharon, her mate, like a puffed-up mother duck.

THE ELEVENTH

BY AMANDA BOYDEN

FUTURE

MIS

We all know that in the beginning, *People* created our heaven and condemned the rest of us to earth. The elders, Fair Shiloh and Dark Zahara, continue to sit lotus as the first ordained. Their brother, Maddox, refused *People*'s calling. His treks across the globe, his alpaca-petting and whale-riding, work in much the same way, but he will never sit lotus. A shame for us. Regretfully, the controversial ruling ten years ago did away with their other siblings' ability to join the sisters in status.

I had the honor of tending Dark Zahara from '22 to '25. Before I came to her, she determined, at the age of twelve, that she would represent the dark continent in mourning colors until the troubles had ended. Now I am a fey old man, but

I must admit, I personally urged her to consider the beautiful side of shadow. My small legacy began with Dark Zahara. Now she wears deep violet like no other, brown and wine and navy, tarnished bronze, silver gone to near black.

My new ward, the eleventh and latest whom *People* has designated Holy, debuts this week. She tips the balance of five female and five male. Everyone waits, zealously, champing at the bit, for our Holy eleventh, Islita. She knows nearly nothing despite my urgings, my hints and nudges. My gut tells me that she lives and breathes not as a product of Love but rather the planning of her very beautiful and A-type-blood-secreting parents. I am certain they procreated with a verbal pre-pro and shook on it, even though all the Holy are supposed to be born of passionate and spontaneous unions. They parted shortly after Islita's mother tested pregnant. Lithe Islita, the ectomorph, knows nothing of the rewards her parents are soon to reap.

DAY ONE

Islita comes out quietly on her eighteenth birthday, as is tradition, but all the earth and heavens watch. There's little to establish, other than her physicality, which I've nurtured for seven months. Islita's appearance is unannounced and choreographed down to the minutiae.

We've chosen a tofu place on the Strip, just popular enough to pass under the radar with enough buzz for a Somebody to notice, a Somebody to get Islita with a cell-cam.

And one does. I see him at his table, eating noodles. He glances, and then glances again. He tries to be sly, tries to be the first. He may get the credit and the money if his cell-cam server is quick enough. And then the crush begins. I whisper in her ear a reminder of her training as they begin to circle, pointing their lenses at the new Holy. Flashes of light fill the room. I know my job for this day is over. Islita's hair, her breast presentation, and her limb ratio will be perfectly represented.

She smiles, her tilted head perfect. She blinks, stands for the followers, for *People,* turns and poses. Good girl, I nod.

I will take credit for this week whether or not I want to. It's in my contract. Tomorrow, she will have her full name. Tonight's debut will determine it.

DAY TWO

Islita weeps. I suspected she would. None of them are ever prepared enough for the weight of it all. But I am old enough to have seen Princess Diana's wedding and her end, old enough to have watched the Hilton empire collapse, old enough to remember Jude Law sober. And so I know how to help Islita. Gentle Islita, they have named her, and she weeps for the passivity of it, for the lack of strength. Her weeping, of course, speaks to her name, and I have to smile behind my hand.

I remind her of her lessons, of Gandhi and Barack Obama. Gentle Islita's tears fill her aqua eyes, spill out onto her mother's cheekbones, collect in the hollows above her clavicles. If this

morning's naming produces such a reaction, I am afraid for
Friday's Flower Ceremony.

It can't be undone, I tell her. It is what it is.

I don't want it, she says, wiping at her eyes. I will need to
apply cold compresses later. Thank goodness for young skin.

I lift her chin, force her to look at me. Gentle, I say, is better than many.

She nods. We cannot change it. She will be Gentle Islita
forever and ever. Amen.

DAY THREE

Today, she goes unbathed in public protest for the Fair Water
Agreement. The move is planned, but I make certain to see
to her appearance, am sure to approximate impulsiveness. She
goes braless, her small nipples hard behind her gauzy shirt.
The shoot takes place in the desert of Nevada. Dry ground.
So much dry ground. The cracks remind me of the lines on
maps.

The cameras snap away, click and click, the photogs clamor-
ing, and I stare at the ground, wondering if the boundaries of
the former Soviet Union are marked anywhere in the earth at
all. Maybe it is only an invisible border of karma alone.

Gentle Islita performs like a trouper. She smiles at me near
the end of the shoot. I smile back, but I have seen the images of
the man for her Flower Ceremony. He will feed the children of
Guatemala for three years for Gentle Islita's hymen. It is not, in

my humble opinion, enough, her blindfold and his anonymity the only saving graces.

DAY FOUR

On her fourth day, Gentle Islita joins the stars, moves from one club to the next. She breaks a shoe strap. A woman from television elbows Gentle Islita in the head. Her casualties are minor, however. I smoke a joint in celebration behind the pool house at night, stare at the moon, and wonder what *People* will print the next morning. The smoke fills my lungs with regret instead.

DAY FIVE

On the fifth day, Gentle Islita says, Today I will fly.

Today you will fly, I agree. Like a bird.

Like a flying fish.

Higher, farther, than a flying fish, I tell her. I am guarding her against tonight. Parachuting, today, will keep her in the moment, for a moment at least.

Later, I watch through the designated screen. My word alone constitutes consummation. I have to watch. I must. Gentle Islita, oh. She does not make a sound. My fist likely does not hide my sobs.

DAY SIX

An elder sends her thanks. At breakfast, we watch Fair Shiloh's message on the wall screen. Gentle Islita scoops at a mango half, her silver spoon tipped with a doe. Her bowl runs with images of elephants, gazelles. She says, I heard you crying last night.

I'm sorry, I tell her.

Why?

Because.

I'm fine, she says. Children will eat for years.

I look at the oats in my bowl, the traditional nudes, the men and women copulating around its ceramic edge. I can't eat.

And that is when it comes, when the wall screen switches to *People Live,* and we see the act as it unfolds.

The man is small and muddy-colored and clutches a knife. He holds an image of Gentle Islita aloft for the crowd to see. He asks of someone to his side, off camera, if *People Live* has tuned in. He appears satisfied with the answer he gets. He kneels. He proclaims his undying love for Gentle Islita. And he slices his own throat.

The screen fills with a torrent of blood, and I know my future will change.

DAY SEVEN

On the seventh day, Gentle Islita rests. She sits lotus, as she must. The chosen followers have paid righteous money to view her live, and she has announced her prayers, as is tradition. The Holy have a success rate beyond question. More than half of their prayers have been answered with the power of *People.* Maddox should be so successful.

Gentle Islita sits lotus, and the people pray for what she wants. She has asked that they pray for understanding and for forgiveness. She is eighteen years and seven days old. And because of the events of yesterday, she is the first to sit lotus behind bulletproof glass at the end of the runway. I see her future and know, beyond question, that she is needed, and she is ready, and she will be lonely beyond belief. I vow to renew my contract. I vow to earn bonuses. I understand my role. I know I will never be Holy by association. I know who I am, and I know what I will be called, forever and ever. Amen.

BLUE MESSIAH

BY STEVE ALMOND

2033

FUTURE

MIS-

Dear Honorable Judge Rheinhorn Reginald Williams,

I am writing, against the recommendation of my attorney Mr.
Geoffrey Planter, concerning my case. As you know, I was con-
victed of twenty-two counts of lascivious assault against Ms.
Teresa Hatch (the plaintiff), along with nine more counts of perversion under God. I believe Mr. Planter's decision not to place
me on the witness stand deprived me of my right to explain my
actions. You struck me, over the course of the trial, as a reasonable
man, perhaps even—if I am reading your eyes right—sympathetic
to my situation.

I entreat your patience.

I am too young to remember when the Great Partition went up, and therefore have always felt a great sense of mystery about how teenagers on the other side live.

As has emerged in court, during a field trip to the Southern Provinces, specifically to the town of Merriam, Kansas, a Spycam 1200 was placed in the alleged victim's room, allowing remote viewing. (I realize that the perpetrator of this crime is a matter of dispute before the court, and I am not about to accuse my alleged friend, Mr. Gregory Goslin, a.k.a. Goose, of having committed this obvious violation of the Surveillance Act of 2027. I will only point out, with all due respect, that I don't even know how the 1200 model works.)

The result was that certain members of Clinton High School were able to establish video contact with the alleged victim, a member of the Church of the Holy Cross Day School's class of 2035.

I have never denied that I viewed the video feed, particularly in the weeks preceding my visit to the alleged victim. But my intention was never lewd in nature. I was simply curious. One hears so many stories about the Southern Provinces: the various restrictions placed on teenagers there, the curfews and mandatory baptismal immersions, the chastity microchips.

Furthermore, as you yourself heard in open court, the actual footage of Ms. Hatch was entirely devoid of sexual content. To quote Mr. Goslin's testimony: "It was boring, man. She just sat at her desk and did her homework and crashed." Another witness,

Mr. Charles Ongoni, a.k.a. Chongo, made the following statement: "We kept waiting. Take the bra off. Something. We got zero."

I later ascertained, from the alleged victim herself, that she wasn't allowed to have friends in her room. As you know, the only time unmarrieds are allowed to congregate in the SP, outside a mega-church setting, is in a retail food sector, such as Ruby Tuesday's or TGIS (Thank God It's Sabbath).

In fact, I continued to watch the video feed for one reason: I sought what I guess I would call salvation.

Let me explain.

Ms. Hatch is not the kind of girl to whom I'm naturally attracted. Her face is plain and she is, if I may be blunt, moderately overweight. I should remind you, also, as my attorney emphasized, that I already have a girlfriend, Ms. Pamela Nicks. Ms. Nicks and I are not only sexually active, we are what one court-appointed expert termed "sexually hyperactive," meaning that we have relations at least three times in the course of any given twenty-four-hour window. I am noting this not to brag, but to provide context. My point is that my toast, sexually speaking, is already pretty well buttered, as it were.

I continued to monitor Ms. Hatch because I found watching her nightly routine compelling. Her serious manner. The way she held her highlighter against the fold beneath her jawline. Her sad little yawns. And, most of all, her nightly prayers.

I do not pretend to be a regular churchgoer, Your Honor. Frankly, living along the Border, and hearing what we do about the Piety Legislation, has led me to question whether religion isn't more a matter of politics than of faith.

But when Ms. Hatch knelt down to pray beside her bed, those doubts melted away. It was as if a great flame had lit inside her. I could see her lips moving. Her eyes turned limpid with yearning. Sometimes, she tilted her head and a flush appeared on her cheeks. And sometimes she would stare directly at me, as if she knew I was out there, watching her, and was calling out to me.

I don't want to belabor the logistics of our eventual meeting. It's easy enough for teenagers to get around the electronic embargo these days. And Border security is flimsy at best, thanks to the Final Shortages. I will say only that the claim that I entrapped Ms. Hatch, or led her down some path of "secular sexual temptation," as the state has claimed, is absurd. You have read the IM records. If anything, a face-to-face meeting was her idea. (To quote, in brief, from defense exhibit #213: "when will i c u? . . . i can't wait 4ever . . .")

There has been a great deal of testimony about the night in question—all false. It is true that I waited until after dark. It is also true that I climbed the trellis to her second-story window. I did so at her instruction, because her mother, I was told, would attempt to kill me if she saw me—a prophecy that, as you know, nearly came to pass.

What was I expecting when I entered her room? I'm not sure. My hope was that we might talk, or perhaps even—it embarrasses me to say this—that we might pray together. My interest in her was spiritual. I realize this may sound far-fetched, given the way I've been portrayed in the tabloid press. But it is the truth.

It was clear to me, however, from the moment I entered her room, that Ms. Hatch had a different agenda. She had lit a number of candles, which exuded an overwhelming scent of vanilla. She laughed nervously and touched her necklace. She spoke in a breathy fashion that did not strike me as natural. Her comments centered on her frustration with her life, particularly the limitations placed on her by the Doctrine of Sanctity and by her mother.

I asked her about her prayers. I wanted to know what she said to God, and how it made her feel.

"But you know already," she said.

At this point, I was sitting in the chair at her desk. She came and took my hand and led me to the bed. "I know who you are." She looked at me again with dreamy intensity. I thought perhaps she wanted to pray right then. But instead, she stood and unbuttoned her robe and let it drop to the floor, so that she was dressed only in her prescribed undergarments. She was breathing quite deeply, her chest rising and falling.

"Might we pray?" I asked her.

"You didn't come to pray—you came to answer my prayers." She did this pouty thing with her lips and stepped toward me through a waft of fruity perfume. "I knew you would come for me." Then she was undressing, her flesh sort of pouring out. She began to sway. "Don't look sad," she said. "You're my blue messiah."

Much has been made of my physical appearance, in particular my alleged attempt to emulate Jesus Christ. I am sure you—and the jury—have seen the various headlines: "Jesus Rapist Strikes Fear in Borderlands." "Sex Savior Attacks Virgin." "The Nasty Nazarene." Etc.

Look, I've worn my hair long and parted down the middle since freshman year. I can't help it that I have a skinny build and a wispy beard and blue, mournful eyes. This is how I look, Your Honor.

Furthermore, the questions I posed to the alleged victim in my instant messages were not, as has been asserted, a "Christly come-on." I did, and do, want to know how it feels to experience the love of God inside my body. I had no intention of whipping Ms. Hatch into a state of lustful rapture.

But that is what happened. She clamped onto me in her state of nakedness and set to clawing at my clothing. She was ravenous, half-crazed, and growling. "Show me the other side." "Make me your bride." Things of this nature.

Given her significant weight advantage, and the tremendous force of her repressed desires, I was left with no choice but to defend myself, which is why, as the prosecutors so eagerly pointed out, I appeared armed when the plaintiff's mother burst through the door, no doubt alerted by the sound of my own head banging against the headboard.

I ask you, would a real rapist attempt to subdue his victim with a curling iron?

Obviously, the senior Hatch chose to heed her daughter's sudden and, if I may say so, totally unconvincing cries of rape. And that is why I stand before you for sentencing.

The ruling of the jury aside, I am an innocent man. My only hope was to understand more about how you in the Southern Provinces live, and how I might establish what Ms. Hatch called "a personal relationship" with Christ.

Despite all that has happened, I can still picture the expression on her face during those minutes she spent, each night, bent in prayer. She struck me as so serene, so assured, something close to free. I do not ask for this blessing from you, as I know it is not yours to bestow. I ask only that you find it within your own heart to spare me the gruesome (and un-Christian) punishments that seem to be called for by the sentencing guidelines.

With all due respect for you, and the truth under God, I remain yours,

Christopher Treybig

IN THE BUSHES

BY JAMI ATTENBERG

FUTURE

MIS-

We met in the bushes. That's where everyone goes nowadays to get their fun on around here, ever since we had to give up the cars. We did it without a fight, because there wasn't much oil left to put in them. The president decided to start a bunch of wars (Q: How many wars can you start at once? A: Four.), and he asked us to donate our cars so we could build weapons, and we all said, "Sure, wasn't like we were using them anyway." And just like that, it became illegal to have a car. They throw people in jails now just for possession of a hunk of metal. So now we walk everywhere, or ride our bikes (the bikes weren't worth their time), and when we want to make out in the backseats of cars, we just use the bushes instead.

I wasn't making out that night. My girl had left me to get married to a soldier who was going off to war. (The one in India, I think.) "No offense," she said. "Benefits." She had met him at one of the barn social nights held just for those purposes—for young women to meet soldiers. I did not know she had been attending them. But marrying a soldier was your best bet for a good life. I could not hold it against her. We had just graduated from high school. I had nothing to give her but a ride on the back of my bicycle.

Although it is a smooth ride.

I was taking the dog for a walk instead, but we were lured by the bushes, the sounds and the smells, the kisses and the moans. Everyone was so happy and free. The air smelled so fresh and green and sexy.

This is what they do now. They start at one end of town at sunset, and, one by one, the kids show up and make the march to the park. By night, the streets are full of kids walking and talking, sharing whatever news they heard their parents whispering about that day. A good piece of dirt can get you laid before dusk breaks. (Not that they're in any hurry: Curfews disappeared with the cars. How far could anyone get? What kind of trouble could they find on their feet?) And then there they are, at last, at the park, in the dark. Kids fall in love in the bushes, babies are made, mosquitoes bite.

Sometimes I miss oil.

They gather near a patch of American elms—that's where

it shifts. Maybe they're thinking about how they're doing their part for our country, our great nation. They swig booze from paper bags, shift from foot to foot. And then they pair off, eventually, wander away from the elms, closer to the bushes, pointing at a constellation, or lying down and hoping for shooting stars. A shooting star guarantees that first kiss. After the first kiss, it's just a short walk to the bushes that spiral up every year higher to the sky.

They've been calling it the Rustle lately.

Not everyone hangs out in the bushes. Some kids like to pair up on a Friday and pick the dirt weed on the back roads. (That stuff was never strong enough to smoke until a few years ago—there was a shift in the air after the explosion in Council Bluffs, and now what looks harmless can send you flying for two days straight.) On Saturdays, the town council hosts a bonfire at the church (mostly old auto magazines); there's romance in roasting marshmallows while erasing the past. And of course there's the equestrians—they're all over the roads. Those girls sure do love their horses; they never seem to want to get off them.

And then there's me. I just like to walk, and watch everyone. When I met her, we were just tracing a little path, me and the dog. I had a stick I was dragging along, and he would stop me every few yards and dig into the ground. She was coming up toward us, a huddle, in the darkness, of sweaters and a sturdy coat and a gigantic backpack. We stopped as we approached and stood in front of each other, and just then a girl let out a loud and very final-sounding moan from the bushes, and the leaves rustled.

"Hi," she said. "I'm lost." She didn't look scared at all, though maybe she should have been, wandering around in the middle of nowhere near all those squirming bodies in the bushes.

"Where are you trying to go?" I said, though I had a pretty good idea.

"I heard there was a place for people like me around here," she said. She shifted her backpack up on her back, and she lifted her head up and the moon and the stars hit her face, and I could see that her skin was clear and her eyes were dark and focused and determined, and then she smiled—not warily, but aware nonetheless. There was a sliver of space between her two front teeth. I wanted to insert my tongue between the space and let it lie there for a while and see what it felt like. The dog liked her, too. He sniffed at her feet and then rested at them.

She was making her way to Los Angeles, she told me. We'd seen a few of her kind passing through before. Los Angeles had seceded from the Union a while back, when the first rumblings of the car reclamation had started. They had fought the hardest out of anywhere. They loved their cars the most. And we had all heard stories of a city trapped in gridlock, but people were still migrating there from all over the country. To a place that still *moved*.

It was a real shame about Detroit, what happened there.

"You're a ways away from the shelter," I told her, but I said I'd walk her in the right direction. It was a nice night. From the bushes we heard two voices jumble together in laughter, and then a guy said, "I love you." I offered to carry her bag for her, and she judged it, judged me, and then handed it over.

As we walked she told me about life back East. Her husky voice perfectly matched the sound of the crunch of gravel under our feet. She had taken hold of my walking stick and dragged it behind her. She was from Philadelphia, and, like every other city out there, there weren't too many trees left, let alone bushes. There were lines every night at the few public parks that remained, and the government charged admission. A fee to flirt. If you couldn't afford that, it was all alleyways for you.

She said she got sick of the feel of cold cement against her ass.

"I know I shouldn't complain," she said. "I know how lucky I am, how lucky we all are. We live in the safest place in the world."

She talked about how much she still loved her hometown, the kind of fun she had there. Young people had taken over downtown Philly with graffiti. When the trees went away, the kids began to paint new ones. People now met and fell in love over a can of paint; five-story marriage proposals covered abandoned buildings. They were calling it a cultural renaissance.

"But I just wanted to see what it was like," she said. She threw her arms up toward the sky and all around. "Out there." She stopped and touched me, turned me toward her. "Not that I care about the

cars so much. Although I guess I do care. What they mean, what
they meant. But I just wanted to be somewhere new."

And then, because I wanted to impress her because she had
impressed me with her ache and desire and energy, even though
I didn't know her at all, even though she could have been lying
about who she was and why she was there, even though I might
never see her again, even though she was tired and dirty and
she smelled of the earth (or maybe because of it), even though I
could have been trading in my freedom, I said to her, "Do you
want to see something really cool?"

We shifted direction toward my home. She dug the trail
behind us with the stick, like we were Hansel and Gretel. We
made it home quickly; we were both excited. I dropped her bag
on the front porch, took the dog off the leash, and let him run
around in circles in the backyard. We walked toward the small
island of trees and bushes behind my house. The dog barked,
nervous, but I ignored him. I held her hand and cleared us a path
through the bushes until we came upon it.

A 2017 Chevy. The roof was missing, and the leather had
been beat down by the rain and snow. Everything else was rusted.
But still we slid in the backseat immediately.

She started to cry, but I think maybe she was laughing, too.

"It's just a useless piece of junk," I said. "It's not that
special."

"No, it's really nice," she said.

I put my arm around her, and we slouched down in the seats and looked up at the sky. "There should be a radio playing," she said. "Classic rock." So I sang, my voice echoing in the trees. I sang her every song I remembered, and then, when I was done with those, I made up a few new ones just for her.

HE

F

EHAVIOR

JAMI
ATTENBERG

PIRATE DADDY'S

LONELY HEARTS CLUB

CALL-IN SHOW

BY JARDINE LIBAIRE

2033

FUTURE

MIS-

FBI-GOOGLE INC. DIGITAL TRANSCRIPT.

RELEVANCE: Red Alert, Hartware Vandals; tracking individuals illegally removing government-mandated software from their persons.

August 23, 2033

[INTRO: DIGITAL-MONOGRAPH SNIPPET OF "PSALM," FROM *A LOVE SUPREME*.]

OPERATOR: [GRUFF, RETRO NEW ORLEANS ACCENT; IDENTITY UNKNOWN.] Well, well, my lions and lionesses, ladies and gents, kids and machines. Welcome to Friday Night Call-in with Pirate Dad-d-d-d-d-d-y. [SPEAKS IN A GROWL.] We're broadcasting in

Digi–crystal 8000 MHz out of the Garage-Prod of yours truly. Coast to Coast. Africa to Ireland. Your hearth to mine, babies. Right now I'm floating over a Replant Onion-grazz Field, and I can see the Western Fire. Yeah, babies, the Western Fire don't show no signs of dying. But that ain't news, is it? [SIGHS.]

I bet a dollar you kids get your news elsewhere, since it ain't my gig, really. But I got this bit for you. Seems we here at WHRT—and by we, lads and lassies, I mean me, myself, and I—are being investigated by FBI-Google Inc. I don't know if you remember the caller from last week, Trinket809. [PAUSE.] Trinket, I don't know if you can hear me. But don't git scared if you can, Trinket. [PAUSE.] She called in to say she was going to dismantle her Hartware. [VOICE CHANGE, DISCOMFORT.] Uncle Sam don't want you to do that, baby girl. [SPEEDS UP.] And I ain't backing up Big Gov. You know Pirate Daddy: I'm a buh–liever in the primitive heart, kitten. But I just can't tell you to go for it, in all good faith, Trink. I can't. [BOOMING.] I'm the man you call to talk to, babes. Call me. It's Digi-Crissy445, through the Floating Japan lines. [RETRO DIGI–SOUND–EFFECT: TELEPHONE RINGING.] Good evening, caller. How's things?

CALLER 1: [PURRING, FEMALE.] Pirate Daddy, well, how do you do. This is Violetbush888.

OPERATOR: [LAUGHING.] Been missing you, Violet.

CALLER 1: [HUSKY WHISPER.] Who can blame you?

OPERATOR: What's the good word, baby?

CALLER 1: I just want to let anyone know who's north of Capital that a lonely little lady is sitting tight at the No-Tell Hotel outside the SleepyMilk Drive Thru. So—

OPERATOR: [CHARMING BUT ADAMANT.] You know the rules, mama.

CALLER 1: *All* I wanna say is, any of you boys get your Milk injection and feel lonely, knock on Prod Digi-Violet. My Hartware is tuned to Twilight Lust, and you know how that goes.

OPERATOR: Violet—

CALLER 1: Daddy, I know! I'm not charging. But that don't make me cheap. [CLICK.]

OPERATOR: That's my Violet angel, making trouble on the digi-waves, like she likes to. [LAUGHS DEEPLY.] Oh, lawdy. Call me, lambs and tigers. Darlings and monsters. [DIGI-RING.]

CALLER 2: [MALE, NASAL, LISPING.] I want to share with your audience my recent Hartware upgrade and its results.

OPERATOR: You braggin' or sharin', baby? [LAUGHS.]

CALLER 2: [UNAMUSED.] I'm *educating.* I just got the Oysterdate Swarovski Settings installed, all hundred. Including [VOICE CONSTRICTED, AS THOUGH WITH SEXUAL FERVOR] the twenty-eight Fetish settings. I can't—I can't find time to try them all.

OPERATOR: [LAUGHS.] Well, this is getting intimate, Jack, but if you're happy, we happy. I mean, about 0.01 percent of our population can *afford* the Oysterdate, but it's cool. Represent for us, baby.

CALLER 2: [BREATHLESSLY.] You're missing rapture—[CUT OFF.]

OPERATOR: That was one flaunty motherlover, am I right? [BOOMING.] Who we got on the lines? [DIGI-RING.]

CALLER 3: [YOUNG MALE VOICE, SCOTTISH ACCENT, JOVIAL.]

Daddy! I just wanted to let you know, yeah, you gave me advice when I called in last week—about the redhead, do you remember? My Hartware said no but my soul said yes?

OPERATOR: How could I forget, honey?

CALLER 3: [SUSPENSEFUL.] Well, guess what? [PULLS AWAY FROM HIS PHONE, PUTS A FEMALE CALLER ON.]

CALLER 4: Daddy, it's me, RedheadToGo5! We're honeymooning fools, and it's thanks to you.

OPERATOR: Awright . . . what do you say?

CALLERS 3 AND 4: [IN UNISON.] We say, "WHRT is where lonely hearts get lost."

OPERATOR: Ha-ha, yeaaahhh. That's what I like. Let the young lead us—you be fearless, cats and kittens. [DIGI-RING.] Who's callin' us from Myanmar, here?

CALLER 5: [STATIC, A COMPUTER VOICE.] Thank you very much for taking my call.

OPERATOR: What goes down in Myanmar, Jack?

CALLER 5: It is hot. Birds sing. The flowers bloom, red and white, delicate, luscious.

OPERATOR: Cool. I dig it.

CALLER 5: I am calling because we passed our Mandatory Hartware Act only three years ago, you might know. I am curious. You in North Americorp passed it in 2017. It is only recently that you have the young people vandalizing themselves, yes?

OPERATOR: [SERIOUS.] Well, what you see on the news is slightly out of proportion, friend.

CALLER 5: But it is true, no, that it is extremely dangerous to remove Hartware, dangerous like the coat hanger procedure done in the mid-1900s? Why are the kids doing it to themselves now? It is because they don't like the Hartware?

OPERATOR: [PAUSES TO THINK; SOUNDS SAD.] No, Jack. Not quite. The kids who were installed at birth, well, they're growing up now, and they want to know what life is like without it. Without a guardrail, you feel me? They never had no say in it, brother. That's making them *act out,* you dig?

CALLER 5: [HESITATES.] My baby daughter was born one week after the act passed. She has had the software in her since she was one hour.

OPERATOR: [MATTER-OF-FACT, STOIC.] You gotta talk to her about it when she gets old enough to understand, brother. Till then, let it ride. [SOFTER.] Ain't nothing you can do till then, sailor.

CALLER 5: [PAUSES, THEN IN GRAVE VOICE.] Thank you for your wisdom, sir. I am grateful. Farewell.

OPERATOR: [TO HIS LISTENERS.] You can't rush it, babies. That's what Pirate says. Who loves me? Who needs me right now? [DIGI-RING.]

CALLER 6: [ELDERLY WOMAN WITH PINCHED, HIGH-PITCHED VOICE.] Is this the Pirate?

OPERATOR: Yes, ma'am, and how can we help your heart tonight?

CALLER 6: [SPITTING.] I don't need your god*damned* filthy hands on my heart, mister.

OPERATOR:Well, don't hold back, Mother.

CALLER 6: I'm calling about these vandals, eh? These self-entitled—do they *know* what it was like before Hartware? Before Pheromone Compatibility Programs, eh? Before Dream Tracker? [SCREECHING NOW.] Eh? Before Hart Fraud Alert? [WHISPERING, SPITTING.] We were in the wilderness. We didn't even know, for chrissakes, what we *thought,* what we *wanted.* We were *lost.* These kids, they have no idea what real heartbreak is. It's no tea party.

OPERATOR: I hear you, Ma—

CALLER 6:They think it's the real thing—"the pure thing," they say. [BITTER LAUGH.] Yeah, well, my grandmother was a girl in the Depression. She didn't *glámorize* collecting jelly jars to me, ya hear? She didn't make like begging pennies was dandy fun.That's what I'm saying. I'm *grateful* for my Hartware.These kids get it free, now, from the government, and they complain? Hell, I worked my hands to the bone to afford my first Hartware.These teenagers now, they make me sick. And you're a shady one.You give 'em this *i-dear* it's okay to go backwards.

OPERATOR:Whoa!? [TRYING TO SOUND AMUSED.] Grandma, you sound like you accusin' me here.

CALLER 6: Calling it like I see it, fella. [CLICK.]

OPERATOR: [SAD LAUGHTER.] Oh, lawdy. [SLOW, LOW VOICE.] Caged-up hearts. Caged up. [PENSIVE NOW.] My Prod is coasting near the Fire, on the Capital side now, and I'm looking down at a Replant Quince-Banana Orchard.Them trees seem to be growing, finally. We gonna be okay, boys and girlies. [PAUSE.] Let's take one more call, lovers, and then we'll put on some sad, sweet song or something, clear our pretty heads. [DIGI-RING.] What have we got on the line for Daddy?

CALLER 7: [VERY SMALL, YOUNG VOICE. CLEAR AS A BELL, BUT FARAWAY.] Hello? [SWIRLING, RUSHING NOISE.]

OPERATOR: I can barely hear you, little sister. [WAITS.] You there? Maybe we should—

CALLER 7: This is Trinket809. I . . . [HUSHING, INCOMPLETE SOUNDS.] . . . did . . . interface.

OPERATOR: [RAW, URGENT.] Trinket809, what'd you do? Did you dismantle it? [SOOTHING BUT DESPERATE.] Trinket, is you *there?*

CALLER 7: [TINY VOICE GETTING TINIER.] I took myself apart, Daddy.

OPERATOR: [EMOTIONAL.] Trinket, Trinket, where are you?

CALLER 7: I'm here.

OPERATOR: Where's here, baby girl? [WAITING.] Do you need help?

CALLER 7: [A LOUD RATCHETING, AND THEN SHUSHING.]

OPERATOR: [QUIETLY.] Trinket, Christ, are you okay?

CALLER 7: I'm alive. [LOUDER WHOOSH, CLICKS, THEN THE CLICK OF THE PHONE.]

OPERATOR: [SPEECHLESS FOR A MOMENT.] I—uh. [VOICE STRANGE.] I'm going to throw a digi-record on the Fonograph here. I'm going to—uh, yeah—I'm going to play this old Chet Baker. "Let's Get Lost." It's going to sound scratchy, babies. [SNIFFS, PAUSES.] But you can hear it pretty true. This one goes out to Trinket809. This is for you, little sister. [MUSIC.]

THE SINGLE GIRL'S
GUIDE TO COMPROMISING
HOMELAND SECURITY

BY JEN KIRKMAN

2033

FUTURE

MIS-

My mom left a book chip—you know, one of those self-help-for-singles book chips—on my unmade rejuvenation platform this morning while I was in the air cleanser. It's bad enough that the New Reform Alien Government has declared single people a threat to planetary security; now my own mother wants me to find a man for all the wrong reasons. "You can grow to love someone," she's always saying. "But for now, just keep a low profile, and get off the New Reform's watch list."

I scanned the chip into my Magno-Electric Information Pad. I was going to have to delete a few more Books on Chip that I never listened to so I could make room for her latest, *How to Marry the Man of Your Choice—And Get Off the New Reform's Watch List!*

I sighed. Humanity has attained world peace, but people who are romantically unaccounted for are considered a security threat. I wished I'd lived before 2008, before other species stepped in to teach us how to live in harmony. I sort of understood their philosophy—that if you spend too much time alone and in your head, it can lead to selfishness and greed, or just sexual frustration, which, in turn, can lead to the desire for world domination—but I refused to believe that someone was a more peaceful person just because they'd found someone to live to be 200 with. And I never thought it was fair that people had to live with their parents until they found a partner.

My mom poked her head into my pod, holding her morning cell-replacement syringe, and immediately started to pry. "You didn't stay late at the Data Dock last night."

"Mother, I'm twenty-one years old," I said. "I'm practically old enough to begin fighting disease with my mind. You don't have to keep harping on my dating life."

"Dating?" she smirked. "That's what we used to say in my generation."

"Okay, okay. Stop harping on my progress to find another human to cohabitate with for the preservation of world peace."

"Just remember," she replied, "if you don't find love, evil wins."

That night, the last place I wanted to go was Speed-Data Referencing. I'd never believed that romance can be found in a warehouse, albeit one that's sterile and completely eco-friendly. I hated walking by other people, holding up my pocket-size

Personal Data Identifier to theirs to check them out. I always walked away immediately to read the results on the screen in private. It was usually the same story: He wants kids, but not until we can procreate with aliens. He loves conspiracy theories—what if the government is in our minds? Or he's almost perfect—he believes in love, conversation, and long walks where the beaches used to be—but he frequently travels to the outer surface of the Sun on the Global Warming Reversal project and will likely be burnt to a crisp before he reaches his first midlife crisis.

But sometimes my PDI will beep, signifying that a match has been made: "Please proceed to the nearest cube corner and begin filling out paperwork. The New Reform Government will contact you both shortly with your first-date assignment, based on your mutual likes and dislikes."

The last time I was at the Data Dock, I saw a guy who was different. He wore jeans, not some kind of hypoallergenic rubber pants like most other men. He wasn't swiping his PDI with anyone else's, which is no small thing. If the New World senses inactivity, a lack of saying yes to life and willingness to date, that's grounds for a visit to an internment camp.

I tried to move my PDI in his general vicinity, to swipe him casually, as if by accident, hoping our compatibility would elicit beeping so wild that the whole warehouse would take notice. But I couldn't get near him. He slinked away expertly, just observing the crowd. We made eye contact a few times, but eventually I lost sight of him. I named him Jack.

JEN
KIRKMAN

My first dates are usually at the restaurant just outside Earth's atmosphere. The view is nice, and with shuttle rates being so cheap, you really can just make a night of it. The conversations are always so seamless it's actually awkward. The guy can usually finish my sentence for me; our compatibility—based on our yearly government-issued personality tests—is so high that we're almost psychically linked. It usually turns out that we work for the same company, Eternal Life, which specializes in defeating human death. Since thousands of people work at this company, it's quite feasible we've never met. But the conversation is always the same.

Sometimes, I just want to pretend to love someone so that I can stop the cycle of tedium. But that would require ripping off the electrodes the waiters fasten to my heart. The last person who took me to dinner was Leo, the humorless bore. He spent the entire night making zero-gravity jokes like "Hey, eat as much as you want. We're weightless!" He said it so loudly the women at other platforms rolled their eyes on my behalf.

But Leo was really attractive. He was one of many babies born whose parents had genetically engineered his physical features somewhere between those of a Greek god and an old-time movie star like Brad Pitt. Listening to him, I wished it were still possible for humans to be deaf, but I tried to make it work just so I could touch him. On my data-analysis form, I indicated that I found him to be funny and charming. But the electrode reading didn't lie. I was fined by the New Reform Government for trying to force something that wasn't meant to be. For nights afterward, when I was alone, I would fantasize about just one night of meaningless sex with Jack back at my pod. But I never got very far. Meaningless sex would get you brought in for questioning—it was an act of defiance against the New World Order.

My mom hates to reminisce about the old days. One morning, I was pulling on my boots as I asked her, "So, you met Dad at a bar? And you just went up and talked to him? And then what?"

"Listen to me," she said, getting up to leave the room. "Nothing was fun before World Peace. We were reckless with our relationships, clinging to anybody we could so we'd never have to be alone. Now, don't stay out all day today. I need help with dinner."

I stepped outside and took a deep breath of the continually recycled lavender-scented air. Riding the solar-powered moving sidewalk to the skyway station, I decided that before I went to the local data station to surrender my reports on how the mating process was going, I'd stop at the Starbucks, one of the only remnants of corporate America. It was overly sentimental to be seen in a place like that, but at least it was legal.

I swiped the tattooed barcode on my wrist on the outside panel of the skyway port and climbed in. It wasn't that crowded, so I was able to sit instead of slipping into one of the awkward Velcro vests and sticking myself to the wall. I teased myself with thoughts of seeing Jack on the skyway. "I'll just go right up to him and talk to him," I thought. "I'll tell him I love him. In front of everyone. I don't care if it's punishable." I let those feelings of anxiety bubble up, giving myself a little rush before returning to reality at my stop.

I walked into the Starbucks and into a world of hipster couples on nostalgia trips. Everyone was sitting at tables, using old-fashioned laptop computers, and drinking coffee out of cups. I became mesmerized by the pastry display, so I didn't see the guy behind me as I stepped back into the line and onto his foot.

It was Jack.

I smiled at him.

"Are you two together?" the girl behind the counter asked. "Ready to order?" I backed off the line, and Jack ordered two coffees. We still hadn't said a word.

He followed me to my table, put the coffee down in front of me, and said, "Hi." I smiled. I wasn't trying to be coy—I was speechless. If this was the feeling that my mom got when she met my dad at a bar, I think it would be worth living in an unsafe world. I checked my PDI; he checked his. They were dark and silent.

He read my statistics back to me. "Works for Eternal Life. Control freak. Overly sentimental. Mildly dissatisfied. Has trust issues." Yup, that was me. Then he turned his PDI off. I looked around nervously. He was going to get in trouble. Within twenty-four hours, someone could come to take him away.

"Don't do that!" I said.

He put his hand on mine and smiled carelessly. "Why shouldn't I?"

I didn't have an answer. "I guess I don't know."

He reached for my PDI. I let him turn it off. "Well, then, I guess we both don't know," he said. He put his hand on mine. I pictured myself jumping over the table and kissing him passionately.

Instead, I reached across the table to shake his hand, even though our left hands were already clasped. I spilled my coffee, reached for a napkin, and spilled his. I had hoped something adorably awkward like that would happen.

"What are you so nervous about?" he asked.

"Oh, I don't know," I said. "Listen, I don't even know you, and I'm risking being taken away by the government just so we can have coffee together."

He laughed. "Come on. You don't believe that, do you? They're not that organized. It's never happened before."

It had never dawned on me that the New Reform couldn't really mobilize. I felt like an idiot. Jack and I might actually have more than a whirlwind romance; we could spend the next two hundred years together.

I glanced across the table and noticed that Jack had one eyebrow hair longer than the rest. He casually launched into a funny story, probably the story he tells on all his first dates when he's on his A-game. I concentrated on that unruly hair, and tried to imagine the day when I'd be comfortable enough to just reach up and pluck it. I hoped that day would never come.

LOVE, AMERICAN STYLE, 2033

BY DARCY COSPER

.

FUTURE

MIS-

By the dawn's early light, the ripe curves of the Capitol dome and the Washington Monument's thrusting shaft gleamed whitely. Sleepy revelers, having streamed out of the city's after-hours fetish discos, oxygen speakeasies, and recently legalized VirtualSex clubs, waited at a heli-bus pad in clusters, examining their enviro-body-suits for damage and blinking up at the Endangered Tropical Lagoon Blue™ scrim of an early spring sky. Nearby, delicate cherry-blossom petals sponsored by the Sovereign Nation of Wal-Mart fluttered like parade confetti onto a lively crowd massed eagerly outside the city's most popular attraction—the National Swinger Hall of Fame.

At last, the front doors to the building swung open, and eager visitors rushed in—pink with anticipation, holocams bouncing around their necks—and hurried to secure tickets for the institution's famous tours and special attractions. High in the lobby's vaulted atrium, above the happy throng, fluttered banners announcing that this year marked the twentieth anniversary of the National Swinging League ("Two Decades of Sharing the Love").

"That's right, y'all. Twenty years!" A pert, ginger-haired tour guide with a Bible Belt twang, the dangerous silhouette of a CybeRockette, and a sleek microphone headset addressed a group of fifty tourists standing beside a life-size titanium tableau depicting the first All-Star Swinging Series champions in their winning configuration, the Twelve-Point Alabama Slammer. "I know it feels like swinging has always been as much a part of the American way of life as it is today." The tour guide paused for effect, looking over the faces of the visitors around her: families with children, young couples, a few foreigners clutching digital translation devices, an elderly foursome on motorized scooters wearing matching golf visors embroidered with the Swinger-World Gated Communities logo.

"You know what's what," the guide winked at them. "You know it's been just twenty short years since swinging was established as a sport with a formal league consisting of only two conferences, eight teams, and no sponsorships! Can you imagine? Only fifteen years since this beautiful building you stand in here was opened to the public as our official Hall of Fame!" Her sweet voice dived and swooped like a tiny honeysuckle-scented roller coaster, all crest and plunge, promise and thrill. "And of course it's been a mere ten years since, by the decree of President Schwarzenegger, swinging was officially declared this great country's national pastime! And if you'll follow me, we're going to learn a little more about the illustrious history of this national pastime. Stay close, please!"

The visitors followed the guide out of the lobby, down a hallway, and into a series of darkened rooms full of luminous, flickering holos.

"Some of you may recognize these images," the guide told her charges. "Can anyone tell me what this one is?" She pointed to the first cluster of holos.

A girl in her teens spoke proudly. "We seen that in my history class last year. That's an episode of *American Swinger.*"

"Exactly right!" the guide said. "As most of you know, competitive swinging began at the turn of the century as a subculture movement. The first sessions we know of took place at swinging conventions, which at that time were quite rare! This early period is well documented in the classic DVD *The Lifestyle II: Keeping Score.* But as the movement gained popularity, secret sessions, sometimes referred to as fight clubs, began taking place all over the country, in underground clubs and private homes.

"Then, in 2009, Robert Evans created *American Swinger*, the world's first competitive-swinging television show, which was broadcast on HBO. A crude but visionary predecessor to competitive swinging as we know it today, the show featured four couple teams in a rotation competition judged by—who remembers? Sir?" She pointed to one of the SwingerWorld residents.

"Dr. Ruth, Hugh Hefner, and Howard Stern," the man wheezed.

"Absolutely right! And in spite of the drug controversy that forced *American Swinger* off the air just five months later, the immense popularity of the show led TeleHongKong, then known as the Fox Network, to develop the legendary show *Swinging with the Stars,* which aired on Sunday nights at nine for eighteen years, ladies and gents! And spawned dozens of swinging-related shows, and got the highest ratings in the history of television." She pointed to a triptych of holos in which naked bodies writhed in rapidly edited sequences.

"Look," a man in his fifties whispered to his wife. "That sequence on the second holo is from the Jude Law–Lindsay Lohan episode. Remember watching that?" He gave her a tender smile, and she squeezed his hand.

"*Swinging with the Stars,*" the tour guide continued, "was almost single-handedly responsible for the widespread interest in and mainstream acceptance of competitive swinging—oh, yes," she nodded at a skeptical-looking young mother with triplets drifting behind her in an Aero-Bassinet. "It's true. The sport initially met with some public resistance, though I know it's hard to conceive of that today! It was also where many of the rules of swinging as we know it today were developed. The eight-couple team, the intra-team exhibition round, and many of the official positions and configurations, all had their origins on *Swinging with the Stars*. For example, the Five-Fingered Johnny, the Elephant Walk, the

Double Dalai Lama, the Green-Eyed Floozy, the Möbius Daisy Chain, the Quadruple Flying Camel—which as you know has been successfully executed just six times—and everyone's favorite, the Octuple Swizzle, among many other maneuvers, were first performed on the show! Okay, everyone, follow me."

The guide led her group through room after room and hall after hall, where they admired elaborate exhibits of equipment and uniforms (The Isaac Mizrahi design worn by Spencer "Toes" Cabot in the 2017 play-offs! The Philippe Starck 2021 commemorative accessory set!); a magnificent collection of Topps National Swinger League Playing Cards (including a rare Ruby Wilson, from her single season in the league, during which she led her team to victory with the first fully executed Triple Sweet Thing and achieved consistently perfect scores in the extemporaneous accessory round before leaving her husband and teammate, Bart, for an antiswinging fundamentalist Sufi); a history of endorsements ("Gatorade, proud sponsor of national champions the Georgia Peaches—is it in you?" "MVP Kelly 'Mouth from the South' Dunn in Nike SwingerWear . . . Just Do It"); a chronology of significant moments (the first NSL advisory board approving the official points-and-penalties guidelines!) and special swinging events (MTV's internationally televised Celebrity Swing Fundraiser for NYC Tsunami Relief! The inaugural Triple X Games!).

At last they arrived at the Hall of Fame itself, a cavernous arcade with floor, curved walls, and vaulted ceiling painted a deep, glimmering crimson. Here, portraits of inductees hung beside cases containing each immortalized swinging couple's trophies and memorabilia. (Sophie and Dan Bluzt of the Seattle Amphibians! Peg and Waldo Springer, creators of the infamous Woolly Mammoth Seizure maneuver! All the members of the 2026 season Detroit Thrusters, the first and only team to achieve a sixteen-way simultaneous orgasm!)

After winding up her discourse on the techniques and triumphs of each inductee, the tour guide paused at the far end of the hall, gently looking at a twelve-year-old boy who was staring with wide, moist eyes.

"Do you want to be a professional swinger when you grow up, sweetie?" the tour guide asked. The boy blushed and shoved his hands into his pockets, and nodded without looking up. "Sure, you do!" the guide said, showing pearly teeth. "We all did at some point, didn't we? I bet you're in Little League, aren't you?" The boy nodded again. "I thought so," the tour guide said. "I was, too, when I was your age! I even went to state in high school. Who here was on their high school swinging team?" About a third of the people in the group raised their hands, and the tour guide beamed and clapped. "That's just great! And who's in a weekend league or on a company team?" More than half of the group raised their hands, including the four retirees. "Well, good for you, guys!" the guide beamed. "That's just super. Yes, was there a question?"

She nodded at a fair-haired young man in his early twenties standing near the back of the group and tentatively waving one hand in the air. Beside him was a pretty, shy-looking girl with dark braids and knee-high silver boots, carrying a digital translation device and whispering in his ear.

"Yes," the young man said. "Please . . ." He turned to his girlfriend, clarified a point in their odd, vowel-rich language, and then looked back at the tour guide. "She please would like to know why your hall has enshrined no great swinging pairs who are man and man, woman and woman. Yes?" The girl nodded vigorously at him and smiled at the tour guide.

A prickly silence descended. A family standing beside the young couple edged away.

"You must be aware," the tour guide said, her voice suddenly sharp, "that the by-laws of the National Swinging Association state that, for eligibility in any official league, every pair of a team must be legally married."

The boy translated this for his girlfriend, who nodded eagerly, bright-eyed, then spoke rapidly in her own language to the tour guide.

"She says to say you," the boy translated haltingly, "that of course, yes, marriage is required for participating in all countries which are being members of the International Swinger League. How is this point relevant to our question that we ask you?"

The tour guide's face flushed crimson. "I'm not sure what country you're from," she told the young couple, her voice tremulous with emotion. "But as every American citizen knows, the 28th Amendment of the Constitution of the United States, passed by Congress on December 2, 2009, and ratified on March 15, 2011, defines marriage as a sacred union between a man and a woman. A man, and a woman."

"Damn right," called out a fat man in a faded T-shirt emblazoned with the words "13th Annual Semi-Pro Swingers Convention, Salt Lake City, 2029."

"Further, American members of the International Swinger League compete internationally *only* with countries that recognize marriage as such," the tour guide continued indignantly. "Iraq. Chile. Vatican City. And the Sovereign Republic of Wal-Mart. Which is why America doesn't send a team to the Olympic competitions. I am proud to say that, unlike those of most countries, our national league is and always has been composed exclusively of opposite-sex couples." The guide's plump lower lip quivered. She lifted her chin and added, "And, I daresay, always will be!"

"Hear, hear," a voice murmured into the ensuing silence as the boy whispered into his paling girlfriend's ear.

"Perverts," someone else hissed. "I bet they're Swedish."

The crowd rustled ominously and shifted in the couple's direction, a soft, hulking animal. The girl drew closer to her boyfriend and clutched his arm.

"Now, folks," the tour guide said, and the mass of bodies lurched back toward her like a cruise ship changing direction. "We've still got quite a bit to see," she trilled at them. "You all follow me, and keep up!" She gave a little wink, then whirled neatly and strode off, her hips twitching from side to side, calling back over her shoulder. "We're going to have to step quick, ladies and gents, or you won't make it to the next showing of our new IMAX presentation, and I bet anything you wouldn't want to miss *Two Decades of the National Swinging League's Greatest Moments,* featuring never-before-seen footage of the best swinging bloopers of all time!"

Surging and shuffling along behind her, the throng departed, leaving the young foreign couple alone in the half dark of the hall, the guide's sweet voice and the footsteps of the visitors echoing thinly off the arcade's crimson walls.

PERFECTION

BY MARGOT BERWIN

FUTURE

MIS-

It was a hard year, 2033. Hard, big tits; hard, flat stomachs; and hard, high-water asses were everywhere.

It was a year of full lips and cat eyes. Small, highly arched feet and firm thighs.

Plastic surgery was subsidized by the government. It was free! And everyone was in on the action.

More and more people were becoming what their minds told them they ought to be, manifesting on the outside what they knew themselves to be on the inside, and the variations were endless. Powerful hormones created a brand-new race of really old children. Always beautiful. Never sagging. Fifty-year-old minds in fifteen-year-old bodies were very popular indeed.

The experimental surgeons got all the glory. No matter how weird you wanted to get, the look was always damn near perfect.

There were specialists in radical surgeries of the face. I, for instance, look like Keanu Reeves, the grand old dude of the cinema, in his prime. I already had the straight, dark hair and smooth skin, so I went for the slightly Asiatic eyes and higher cheekbones. I'd always felt my life would be better if I looked like he had as a young leading man, and, you know what? It is. I love being Keanu Reeves, even without the talent, the money, or the actual genetics.

My girlfriend Ava had the look du jour. She was naturally slender, or so she told me, her fake breasts were like two round teacups, and her teeth were whiter than white. She'd had the requisite work done, and she was, quite frankly, perfect. And that's where the problems began. Unfortunately for me—and for her—perfection simply did not do it for me.

"You're never happy anymore," she said. "What can I do to myself to make you happy?"

"I want to have sex with a lot of different women," I said. "And, just to be completely clear, I want to feel different holes."

I knew I sounded like an ass, but I didn't know what else to say. I couldn't ask her to undo herself.

As you can imagine, Ava wasn't too keen on me sleeping with different women, so she came up with a pretty good solution. A damn innovative one, truth be told. She asked our plastic surgeon to create a few more holes in her body.

Technically, they wouldn't be described as holes, exactly, but rather flaps of skin, undetectable to the naked eye, housing sloping indentations in fatty parts of the body, replete with nerve endings.

Our doctor was more than happy to oblige, as it was a brand-new technique, not particularly risky, and very likely to get him a double-page spread in the next edition of *JAMA*.

At first, it was a joy, but in the end, Ava was a typical hard body: Hard breasts. Hard butt. Hard bone structure. And I was so tired of bone on bone. I wanted fat on bone. Hips I could grab on to.

Everything I used to get off with was ancient history—books and videos filled with people who look like people used to look. I loved old Andrew Blake DVDs and *Perfect 10* magazines. It was somewhat of a fetish of mine, those imperfect folks from a bygone era.

I guess that's why I found myself peeking into the bathroom across from mine at the woman with the lined face. Not even my grandmother had lines in her face anymore. I couldn't tell how old the woman was, because hardly anybody looked old, so I had no basis for comparison. She could've been thirty-eight. Or fifty. To me, it didn't matter in the least. She wasn't perfect, and that's what counted.

I was heading back to my flat for another night of bone-on-bone action with Ava when I met my neighbor in person for the first time. It was a bit of a lucky accident, as I noticed that her keys were still in the door. I took them out and knocked, and when no one answered, I pushed it open just a little bit.

I stood in her doorway like an idiot and stared. She was in big white panties, watering her plants.

Everything was in the wrong place.

Her breasts were not facing her chin like those on the women I knew. They were soft and full and hanging downward. I wanted to walk over and lift them up and hold them against her in a more comfortable position.

Her stomach was not flat or defined, but round and soft and sloped, her belly button closer to her bladder than to her stomach. Even her knees were low-hanging.

She looked me over.

"I've seen you looking through the window," she said, pointing at the bathroom with one hand while still watering the plants with the other. I was amazed at her lack of fear at my standing in her doorway.

"You left your keys in the door," I said.

"Bring them to me."

I walked toward her, holding the ring of keys out in front of me like a sleepwalker.

"What do you think about when you look at me through that window?" she asked, bending over a ficus tree and touching the soil.

"I think about how sure of yourself you must be."

"Because I've never had any work done?"

"Yes," I said.

She looked between my legs. I was afraid to look down.

"What else?"

"I think about how soft you look," I said quietly. "And I think about what you might feel like."

She came closer, taking the keys with one hand and putting the other between my legs.

"I think about you, too," she said, as she sat down on the couch in front of me and brought my pants down around my knees. "I think about all of you, all of your kind. And I feel sorry for you. So sorry."

She reached between my legs and held me with her breasts, something most women could not do anymore because of the implants. Her softness was shocking. I moved back and forth, in and out of her realness, with my eyes closed.

I lay down on my back and she sat on top of me, her breasts swinging freely back and forth like they were meant to do. When they stopped, I tapped them on either side so that they would do it again. I could have watched them sway like that forever.

I gathered up her belly skin, pulled it apart, and draped it around her waist. There was so much to hold onto, I felt like opening up her skin and crawling inside.

Later, back in my own place, I thought of all that softness living right down the hall.

To me, she was a rare, exotic find. Like a dinosaur bone to an anthropologist, or a Virgin Mary sighting on the side of a barn in Nebraska.

She didn't need the extra holes, like my girlfriend did. Her entire body was one big, soft, pull-able, sink-in-able hole.

"What are you doing in the bathroom?" Ava called to me.

"Nothing," I lied, staring at my neighbor, ready to put my hand through the glass of both windows just to touch the lines on her face.

AUTHOR
BIOGRAPHIES

Steve Almond is the author of the story collections *My Life in Heavy Metal* and *The Evil B.B. Chow and Other Stories* and the nonfiction book *Candyfreak*. His most recent book, *(Not That You Asked): Rants, Exploits, and Obsessions,* will be published in late 2007. To find out what kind of music he listens to, check out www.stevenalmond.com.

Jami Attenberg has written about sex, technology, design, graphic novels, books, television, and urban life for Salon.com, *Print, Nylon,* and the *San Francisco Chronicle*. Her debut collection of stories, *Instant Love,* was published by Crown/Shaye Areheart Books in June 2006. A novel, *The Kept Man,* will be published by Riverhead Books in 2007. She lives in Brooklyn. Visit her at www.jamiattenberg.com.

Margot Berwin is the author of *Irresistible,* a work of creative nonfiction. She is currently working on an instructional novel called *How to Avoid Disaster.* She lives in Manhattan.

Amanda Boyden is the author of *Pretty Little Dirty.* She lives in New Orleans.

Darcy Cosper is a writer and book reviewer. Her work has appeared in publications including the *New York Times Book Review, Bookforum, Village Voice, Nerve,* and *GQ,* and in the anthologies *Full Frontal Fiction* and *Sex & Sensibility.* Her first novel, *Wedding Season,* was published by Crown in March 2004. She lives in Los Angeles and New York.

Ana Marie Cox is the creator of the Washington-based political blog Wonkette. She is a columnist for *Time* and Time.com, and the author of *Dog Days.* She is at work on her next book, an anthropological study of young conservatives. She lives in Washington, D.C.

Lisa Gabriele's writing has appeared in the *New York Times Magazine, Vice,* the *Washington Post,* and on Salon.com and Nerve.com. She directs and shoots documentaries for the Life Network, the History Channel, and the Canadian Broadcasting Company. Her first novel, *Tempting Faith DiNapoli,* was published by Simon & Schuster. She lives in Toronto, where she's at work on her second book.

Karl Iagnemma's writing has appeared in *Playboy, The Best American Short Stories,* and *The Journal of Autonomous Robots.* His first book of short stories, *On the Nature of Human Romantic Interaction,* was recently published by Dial Press. Visit www.karliagnemma.com for more information.

Jen Kirkman is a writer and comedian. She has appeared on numerous TV shows, including Comedy Central's *Premium Blend,* NBC's *Late Friday,* and Oxygen's *Hey Monie!* She also performs live at the Hollywood Improv, the Laugh Factory, the M Bar, and the Comedy Central Workspace. She lives in Los Angeles.

Walter Kirn is a contributing editor to *Time* and a regular reviewer for the *New York Times Book Review.* His work has also appeared in the *New York Times Magazine, GQ, Vogue, New York,* and *Esquire.* He is the author of four previous works of fiction: *She Needed Me, Thumbsucker, Up in the Air,* and *My Hard Bargain: Stories.* He lives in Livingston, Montana.

Jardine Libaire holds an MFA from the University of Michigan. Her stories have been published on Nerve.com and in *Fiction* and the anthology *Chick Lit. Here Kitty Kitty* is her first novel. She lives in Brooklyn.

Tom Lombardi's fiction is forthcoming in *McSweeney's Quarterly,* and has appeared in *Fence* and *Opium* and on McSweeneys.net. His Web site is www.tomlombardi.org.

Jay McInerney is the author of the novels *Bright Lights, Big City; Ransom; Story of My Life; Brightness Falls; The Last of the Savages;* and *The Good Life.*

Rick Moody's most recent novel is *The Diviners.* His other books include *The Ice Storm, Purple America, Demonology,* and *The Black Veil.*

Douglas Rushkoff is the author, most recently, of *Get Back in the Box: How Being Great at What You Do is Great for Business,* and the new Vertigo serialized graphic novel, *Testament.* He founded the Narrative Lab at NYU's Interactive Telecommunications Program.

Will Self is the author of five novels, four collections of short stories, four novellas, and three non-fiction collections. His most recent novel, *The Book of Dave*, was published in 2006 by Bloomsbury USA. He lives in London with his wife and four children.

Rachel Shukert is a playwright, performance artist, and actress who can often be seen in New York if she is not in Europe, where she wastes a lot of time. She is the cofounder of a soon-to-be-legendary theater company, the Bushwick Hotel. Her work can be read at Culturebot.org.

Joel Stein is a columnist for *Time* magazine.